DEATH'S QUEEN

JANEAL FALOR

ISBN: 9781946860002

Cover by Lou Harper

To learn more about this author, visit: janealfalor.com

BOOKS BY JANEAL FALOR:

Mine Series

Mine to Tarnish (Mine Prequel)

You Are Mine (Mine #1)

Mine to Spell (Mine #2)

Mine to Fear (Mine #3)

Sacrifice of Mine (Mine #4)

Darkening Light

Ever Darkening (Darkening Light #1)

Savage Light (Darkening Light #2)

Elven Princess

Bound by Birthright (Elven Princess #1)

Bound to Endure (Elven Princess #2)

Bound by Love (Elven Princess #3)

Standalone

Goddess Ascending

A Genie's Heart

To Erik
For loving me in the darkest of times

CHAPTER 1

"You will kill who I tell you to kill." Daros's voice is low. Threatening.

My insides quiver. I'm not the type to stand up to my master. He's not just larger than me; he also holds such power over me that I shake to think about it. Yet after everything I've seen, stand up to him I must. "No. No more."

He comes around his massive desk, forming a fist. "What did you say?"

"I will not kill for you."

He steps up, his favorite jeweled dagger in hand, pressing it against my throat. A man enters the room, and Daros gives a quick glance at him before turning back to me.

"I don't have time to deal with this." He snaps his fingers. "Go up to your room. Consequences will come later, but know you will do what I say. That's the only reason I ever took you in to begin with."

I slink away, unrepentant, passing by the unfamiliar man. No matter what he says, I'll never kill again.

It might be harder if he takes me into *the* room.

Still, after last time, I'm determined to stand free. To not do it again.

The house is as grand as ever, even if I am not in Daros's good graces. I wish I could get my hands on one of the many hundreds of books I pass, but there's no touching Daros's things, especially books. I hurry my way through the house toward my room. The swirling wooden staircase is silent beneath my steps. I don't touch the carved banister. If I can't get up the stairs without touching it, I've got bigger problems than falling down.

At the top, I move toward another, less lofty, staircase. As I climb, the thought of leaving comes to me. The house is empty of all others except guards. I'm the only assassin Daros owns. The only person foolish enough to stay.

Not that he's given me other options.

He hires a handful of assassins from time to time, but I'm his tool. Or I was. I no longer wish to remain so. I've thought of this before, but not with such vigor.

I open the door to my room. It's sparse—only a few blankets on the floor. I plunker down on them and let my idea stew. Should I really leave? This is the only roof I've known over my head. Until now, Daros's threats and punishments were enough to keep me here.

If I go, there will be no more shelter. No more food. But then, there will be no more killing. No more following his orders.

Ever since I can remember, I've either been training to kill or killing for him.

The world outside isn't a kind one. It will be hard to get food. Hard to find shelter. Hard to find a useful life, according to Daros. But is a life really what I want?

After all I've done, I'm not sure I deserve it. I'm sickened, except for the parts of me that are hollow.

I open my window and look outside. It's a beautiful street, full of neatly arranged Kurah class houses. The rich can find no better neighborhood than this, unless they go to the palace.

The stones used to make the Kurah houses glimmer in the light. A cobblestone road with grass in front of the buildings and precise lines lies in front of the homes. There's a faint scent of flowers in the air. Nothing to match the turmoil inside my soul.

The ledge outside the window is meant for decoration, but I can climb on it easily. It wouldn't be the first time, but it may be the last. I've been here all seventeen years of my life that I can remember. Is now the time to leave? Yes. I believe it is.

Decision made, I grab my daggers and stash them on my person. Once they're situated, I check to make sure my pouch of poisons and antidotes is hanging around my neck. Its presence is a bittersweet reminder of things that are in my control—which aren't many.

I swing out the window and creep along the wall, sticking to it like a spider. I shimmy down the wall and use stones that are jutting out when I reach the corner of the house.

It's this part that's dangerous. If Daros looks out the window and sees me, I'll be lucky if I get an arrow to the shoulder. I can't go back. Can't return to the room of horrors.

I breathe in and out three short times to find my courage and make a break for it. Once I get to the cobblestone street, I slow to a walk.

Somehow, I made it away from the house.

Then I hear a shout. Fear punctures my lungs, making it hard to get air.

One of Daros's guards is headed after me. The pounding of my heart matches the pace of my feet on the ground. He'll give chase as long as it doesn't draw attention. I've got to get to people.

Still, escaping this guy won't matter.

Daros will know how to find me.

Fear pushes me harder. Makes me stronger. Faster.

I weave through the streets, my back burning with his gaze. He is fast, but I am lighter. Swifter. At least, that's what I tell myself.

I swing to a street on the right, my feet slapping against the stone path beneath me. Houses seem to fly by as I run, each different than the last. The sunlight is bright. I should have left at night. Or maybe I shouldn't have left at all. But if I go back now, Daros will torture me. Scar me with his hatred.

I push forward, toward the market, swerving through several more streets. A glance over my shoulder shows no one trailing after me, though others are on the street, most headed the same way as me. Still, nerves claw at my chest. He could be coming in at a different angle, to head me off.

I turn down another street, and the market comes into view. I hasten to it. I've done it so many times before, but always on Daros's errands. Thinking of the jobs he's sent me on makes me shudder.

Pushing the thoughts aside, I follow the flow and get lost in the crowd. Numbness consumes me. Fills me to the brim with its frigidness.

I seem to have lost the guard for now. This doesn't mean I'm clear. There are still ways Daros could follow me. Find me. Torture me. Force me to kill for him again.

I clench my jaw. I've been trained to play a part. It won't be hard to act like I'm living off the streets. If only I'd learned something about Daros, all that time at his house—a secret to give me an advantage over him...

But there is nothing.

His secrets were as tightly held as I was. Though, if I can escape, maybe someday his secrets will too. Not that they're my concern any more. For now I need to focus on staying out of his clutches and away from being tormented.

Night is coming on. They'll be sure to light the pathways by the palace of the dead queen, but there's no such luxury toward the slums where I'm headed. I've been to both places many times. This city is familiar to me. I had to know it to do my job. Now I will no longer be sent on errands. It doesn't give me as much comfort as it should.

The cobblestone gives way to packed dirt. It's easier to silence my steps on it. First order of business is finding somewhere to sleep tonight. Not that I'm tired, but I don't feel like wandering the streets all night.

Watching my back will be much easier from a place I can control. Though it might not be worth the effort. What's the point of my existence?

I have nothing to offer.

The smell is foul down here, like no one has ever cleaned the place or put in a sewage system. Why would they? Daros says beggars aren't worth taking care of.

There are plenty of Poruah out, old and young, many of whom are staring at me. Most are dirty with the muck of the day. Lots of girls in skirts and boys in pants. I go to a girl who looks about my age. She won't stop staring at my clothes. Hers are tattered bits of brown cloth, but she's one of the few wearing pants like me.

"Trade outfits with me," I say.

"Why would you want to do such a thing? Mine are terrible, and yours are so… nice."

"My father beats me. If he finds me down here, it will be worse for me. Your rags will help me hide." It might as well be the truth, though Daros certainly isn't my father and a beating would be the least of my troubles.

She nods. "I know a place we can switch."

I follow her behind a shack that's presumably someone's house —maybe hers. It looks as though a big wind would knock it over. As long as it stands while I change, it's not my concern.

The girl changes clothes with me. She takes my white shirt and gives me her brown one that's stiff with grime. Her clothes are coarse against my body. I reach down and smear dirt across my face and mess up my short brown hair. Daros will recognize me, but it won't be as easy.

"If you come with me, I can show you someplace safe to sleep," the girl says.

Her sweet tone makes me wonder what she's hiding. Why is she helping? What could be to her benefit? Still, I contemplate her offer. Being among others would make me harder to find, but it's not my place to be with others.

"I can make it from here." I make my voice cold.

She gives me a funny look but hurries on her way.

When I come out and walk along the river, no one looks at me. I fit in.

A week of my life goes by in a numb stupor. I planned on getting a job—anything besides killing. Something where Daros couldn't use me. I thought I could put the past behind me. Thought I could move on. But as time passes, the more I realize I'm not entitled to survival. Not entitled to anything.

I never was. I just didn't see it before, being Daros's drone.

I can't move on.

The faces of those I killed haunt me.

I want to disappear.

To become nothing.

The truth is I gave up my right to live when I stole that right from others. There has to be something I can do about it.

The bleakness in my chest pounds at me. I don't speak to the other homeless people milling about the dirt-paved streets. Don't acknowledge their presence.

Now that I've killed so many for Daros, my life is no longer worth anything. I've had more kills than I can count. Many more than I should have. I've heard whispers about me. That death comes to many by secret means. That the Shadow Wraith kills in one blow, when you least expect it.

No one knows who will be next or why. Not even I. Only Daros does.

The guilt has clawed at me for some time, but only now, when I have so much time on my hands do I realize how severe it is. It's choking, bloodying its way through me.

I reach the market again. Being in the capitol, it's huge compared to others, I'm told.

Voices are calling out a jumble of things.

"Fresh fish. We catch, you cook."

"Cotton, wool—we have it all."

"Buy a pretty bracelet for your pretty girl."

"Roast chicken. Get your roast chicken."

"Carvings of all types. Women. Animals. Landscapes. You name it, we can make it."

Adding on the sound of customers chatting, and it's a cacophony. It's overwhelming to be against such a rush. The noise feeds my senses, drowning out my fears. For the moment.

There's an odor in the air, like the place hasn't been cleaned in a while. Over that is the smell of roasting meat. The stalls have so much food, fruits, vegetables, and more. I was little, but I remember the famine. The pain in my stomach becomes stronger at the memory.

I have no money. I could steal an apple, but it doesn't matter.

I don't deserve to eat.

Don't deserve anything but the numbness in my soul.

I pass the food carts, stop, and stare at a jewelry vendor. The wares on the wooden table are elegant and refined. Bracelets with pearls from far-off oceans. Necklaces with rubies and diamonds. Rings with sapphires. They're all so sparkly and bright.

I reach out to touch one. Not to steal it—I have no need for fine things, nor do I deserve them. Just for once, though, I want to see what they're like. If they're hard, like the fake ones I wore on certain jobs. If they're cold against my skin.

"Get your slimy hands away from my merchandise," a woman covered in her own jewels shouts. "Get out of here, before I call the law."

For a moment, I'm tempted to stay. What if the lawmen did come? Would they take me away? Would they hang me or cut off my hand for attempted stealing? It's a harsh punishment that isn't usually doled out, but I've earned it.

But no. I take a step back. And then another.

I could handle the pain, but why bother? Daros would be sure to find me at a public hearing. One of his minions would tell on me. I won't go to him, to be tortured and put back into his service. To be the Shadow Wraith.

I make my way past other vendors, barely taking them in. I have to will to care about them.

The crowd thins as I move past the market, but there are still people milling about. I pass a few people spotted with almaca, a disease that will kill them for lack of food. Or perhaps it's the poor quality of food. All I know is these people are lucky. They'll be escaping this dreaded life soon.

I walk, misery shrouding me. I pay little heed to what I'm

doing. Where I'm going. Until I realize I'm headed to Daros's house. My feet must have instinctively gone this way. For torture?

No. I don't want that. I hurry away, paying better attention to where I'm traveling.

"You, there," a thin but muscular man calls out.

I glance around. He's calling for me. This is it, then. Daros has found me.

I'll be hauled back to his house, to be tormented. Starved and tortured. Hated. And if he doesn't think I've repented after that, it will be my death.

A blessed darkness.

But only an *if*.

"Do I know you from somewhere?" the man asks.

I should run, but my feet won't move.

He doesn't look familiar, but that means little. I know many faces from the many jobs I've done. "No," I say.

He narrows his eyes as he leans in closer. "I swear I know you from somewhere."

My heart should be racing now, my mouth going dry. None of the usual fear sensors are going off. I'm numb. I don't want to go back, but apparently not enough to send me into caring.

"Huh. Get on with you, then." He brushes past me, heading toward the direction of Daros's house.

It's easy to return to my mindless wandering. I tell myself not to go to Daros's, but other than that, I don't care. I just can't.

There's a gnawing ache in my chest. Something I can't control or do anything about. Well, there is one thing, but it would be the final thing I'd ever do.

My feet are silent against the cobblestone. The noise of people comes in the distance. Despite myself, I'm drawn toward them. It's a nicer area here—strips of park, covered with trees and flowers. The crowds are dressed in fine things, and many people give me dirty looks, but it doesn't matter.

I reach the palace and find numerous people going through the portcullis and inside the impressive building. But of course—it's the day for the Death Drink. Drinking the Mortum Tura either kills

8

you or—rarely—makes you queen. The opportunity to try it comes once a week since we lost our last ruler. It's luck I stumbled this way on the day the drink is to be taken by those who chose to risk it.

What better way to ease myself out of life than with the famous drink? I could kill myself a million ways, but this way would be brave. The way all women are supposed to try. No more waiting for death to find me. I'm coming to it.

CHAPTER 2

I PUSH my way through those moving toward the palace until I'm almost at a run. The white of the building blurs together in a mesh of colors as I rush inside. People tumble around. Elbows are thrown. Legs try to tangle me.

Nothing can stop me from getting to my goal.

I dart through the huge open doors, past the guards, and to the first chamber I come to. It's a huge room, with mirrors for walls. The floor is a gleaming oak with numerous people treading on it. There are still others about, but the crowd isn't as thick.

Up ahead, I see a chalice up on a pedestal, surrounded by a bunch of girls, women, and one man. That's my destination.

A flicker of doubt goes through me. Do I really want this? I push it aside. Of course I do. I've never been so sure of anything before.

As I make my way to the back of the group of girls, the man says, "I am Ranen, the Head Advisor of the late queen. I'm in charge of the Mortum Tura this day. We will begin shortly." His voice is reedy, and he has a tasseled hat and well-rounded body. His dark eyes take in those gathered but glaze right over me. He's the type of man that thinks he's above anyone else by the way he holds himself and ignores me.

I push my way forward. I haven't drawn attention to myself like this before. I was always a whisper, instead of a shout. But now I have to shout if I'm to get the drink. What's more, I won't wait.

I need it now.

Some of the girls glare as I move past them. Some look relieved, while others try to bar my way. Much stronger than them, I shove my way through. When I get to the front of the group, where Ranen is standing next to a dais, I yell, "I will take the Mortum Tura."

Ranen sends a thick glare at me. He opens his mouth to speak, but I ignore him. Nothing will stop me. Not this man. Not all the pristine, well-dressed girls around me. Not my own fears.

I take a step up. The dark stone pedestal is etched with the names of those who came before me and failed. I will soon join them.

With a huff, Ranen says, "Fine. Drink."

And then it's up to me.

One taste—that's all that's between me and death.

Failing to become queen now means I'll never fail again. Which is what I want. It gives me some comfort, albeit the coldest kind. The crowd around me watches eagerly, hungry for my death, yet hoping for my life. Hoping for the next Queen. There are many of them in the grand hall of the palace. Enough to almost fill the entire room. Despite their number, those gathered are silent. Everyone's waiting to see what happens.

They've been without a queen since the last one died a month ago. She reigned for almost five years, and her death was a mysterious one to the general public. The palace hasn't released a reason for it.

Typical. Queens' lives are often threatened by one force or another. Another reason not to become a royal, though I don't need more.

My choice is to die.

The anticipation of having a new, long overdue ruler doesn't diminish the crowd's excitement. The prospect is not nearly as entertaining as that of my agonizing death—the slow, torturous kind.

Why am I picking this again?

Right—because even a slow, torturous death is better than letting Daros have me. Better than living life as a ghost, alone and cold.

For a few long moments, the world cares about what I'm doing, and then it will be over. I'll have gone out trying to fulfill a duty all females have been asked to do but few try, because of the fear of death. We are free to choose whether to drink or not, despite being asked.

If I had a name, it'd soon be etched into the stone pillar holding the chalice of death or I could be given full control over a country. Things have been like this as far into history as I know. When one queen dies, another is found through the Mortum Tura, to take her place. Many die, but one lives and becomes our new ruler.

And now it's my turn for one or the other.

Either way, I will be remembered.

"It's time," Ranen says, the tassel of his hat swinging in rhythm with his irritation. *Past time*, he means. He doesn't want me to try; urchins off the street shouldn't dirty the chalice with their touch. They shouldn't try for the Mortum Tura. Of course, he has no choice but to let me. All unmarried women have the choice—even dirty ones.

In my defense, I would have cleaned myself, had I realized what I was doing.

I grasp the pewter stem. This is for the best. I'm done with life, and there's no better way to go out, despite the fact it's painful.

Only thing is I'm having second thoughts. Not about death, but about torture. How bad is it going to hurt? I'm used to pain, but there are quick, painless ways to die. I know many. Why'd I have to pick this one?

They say the last girl to try to become Queen screamed for a full day before she finally gave in to the next life.

It's not exactly the end I have planned for myself, but I should have thought of that before I came before this crowd. I won't be a coward and back out now.

Death, I'm coming.

I press the cup to my lips and swallow the maroon liquid. It's sweet, like the pomegranate seeds dipped in chocolate I once stole when I was a child.

Who knew death would be such a treat?

Trying to be as graceful as I can in my last moments, I set the chalice back on its pedestal. The pain will be coming soon, and the cup will refill itself, readying for its next victim—the next to try and claim the throne. Not that I ever wanted the throne; having everyone watching me is enough. And I don't like it as much as I thought I would.

The people's eyes are black with hunger for entertainment of the cruelest kind. The girl that survives the Mortum Tura to become queen will have a trial getting such people to follow her rule. Or maybe they'll be so eager for leadership, they'll drop whatever they're doing to worship her.

I will never know, as I won't be around.

Is that a pricking in the back of my throat? Is it the start of my drawn-out death? Hurting would be feeling something, which is better than the hollow ache eating away inside me.

But no, it's a tickle in my throat. Nothing else happens. No hurting. No crumbling to the floor. No blood pooling out of me. No screaming.

I only want torture.

Pain.

Release.

Perhaps it hasn't been long enough?

When I glance at the plump Ranen, my thoughts change. He widens his eyes with each passing second, as if he can't believe what he's seeing before him. The crowd's gaze has changed from hunger to awe. First one man kneels, pressing his face to the wooden floor. Then another. And another. Soon, everyone is on the ground. Even Ranen.

A mirror on the far wall shows me why they hold me in such awe.

I am glowing.

Golden and bright, my entire being radiates magnificence. They think me a goddess.

But I am not.

I'm just an assassin, ready for death.

CHAPTER 3

THE CROWD STAYS prostrate before me for a time that's hard to fathom. The only sound I know is the drip, drip, dripping in my head. I don't know what it is, but it's the most determined thing that's ever been in my life. I'm determined to go back to seconds ago, when I thought this was still a good idea, and change my mind. Before I survived the Mortum Tura.

What am I to do with these people? I can't rule over them.

I cannot be Queen of Valcora.

This can't be happening.

The stunned silence creeps over me like fog stealing through the night air. How does a death wish, a guaranteed death sentence, turn me into the ruler of a nation?

I should have picked another way to die.

Still the people remain prostrate before a girl who moments ago was only entertainment. And before that? Nothing worth remembering.

But I do remember. The harshness remains at the forefront of my thoughts. If the people knew, they'd have even less of a reason to bow before me. I've been trodden on my whole life, Daros demanding whatever he wanted of me. That can't change now, just because of the Mortum Tura.

Why do they remain bowed? Why don't they get up?

It dawns on me I haven't given them permission to rise. Of all things, they're waiting for me. This doesn't seem possible.

"Get up." I don't know what other words to use, though those two feel clumsy and wrong for this purpose of commanding the people.

As one, the people do so, but they do not disperse. They stare at me as if waiting for another command.

What am I supposed to do? I know nothing but stealing and stabbing. And poisoning. And sword fighting. Fine—I know more than I like to give myself credit for, but I know nothing of such things as leading a people.

I've no one to go after now. I'm the one who wants death.

I want them gone. I want to be out of the light. Out of their lives. "You can all leave," I say, silently pleading they do so.

Not one of them moves. Their gazes stay riveted on me, until *finally* those farthest from me begin to trickle away like a stream that babbles until it rushes away. Though unlike with a stream, there are too many backward glances.

I give nothing away.

I'm expressionless.

Emotionless.

Empty.

When everyone's left except Ranen and a few men and women around him, Ranen says, "Forgive us for not obeying." Despite his words, his voice tells me he's used to being the boss and expects to remain so. "We would like to guide you through your new role and help you understand what to do next."

Whether I should be relieved or not remains a mystery. I think not. He disliked me the moment I declared I was going to try the Mortum Tura. Why would my becoming the queen change that? Besides, I distrust his shifty eyes.

Queen. That's what I am now.

It doesn't seem real.

I realize he's still waiting on me for an answer. "Go ahead."

He bows his head. "If Your Majesty would follow me."

16

I grit my teeth over the honorific. Ranen leads me out of the chalice room and through a blank hall. Even the floor is oddly white, though at the next corridor we reach rugs are on the floor, plusher than any I've ever felt before. There are pictures on the wall—lovely landscapes of Valcora that barely hold my interest. The only beauty I see is cold. Calculating. The steep slope of the mountains around us trying to keep us in. To close us off from the rest of the world. Keeping us cut off when the famine abounds.

"It would be best if you came to me when you need something," he says. "In fact, it would be even better if you left everything up to me. I've been taking care of this country since our last queen died, and I know how to run it properly."

I have a feeling I'm going to dislike this guy more than I already do. I don't care about running a country, but I do care about his attitude. I've had enough of Daros in my life; I don't need another like him.

The palace is ornate, filled with drapes of highest quality and pictures of nobility. The hallway is airy and bright, with lots of windows and a tall ceiling. The stone walls seem to amplify the light instead of absorbing it.

"The first thing we need to do is clean you up. Dress you in something befitting royalty, instead of a…" He looks me over, face scrunched. "Your rooms are down a few more hallways, where your servants will be waiting. They are new. No one has stayed in them before."

I have servants? I can't imagine what that'll be like. I've always taken care of myself. I'd prefer it remain that way. Others can't be trusted.

We pass several servants, dressed in light blue and scurrying through the halls, who aren't as plump as Ranen, but are clearly well fed. I think of my bony body matching most of the Poruah class and can't help but keep my gaze down. Daros kept me fit enough to do my job, but nothing more. Starved only sometimes. Mostly, I was fed protein. It left me thin but strong. At least I have that on the lowest class of people.

If only I'd gotten a job as a servant when I was little, things would be so much different.

Not that I had a choice.

After a long walk in silence, with several twists and turns, we stop at a door.

"These are your rooms," he says. "Your servants will attend to you, and then I will see to your training."

He almost glares, which is unnerving, so I hurry through the door, only to be met by a woman who ushers me through the room to a second room. It is airy with a vaulted ceiling, and half a dozen well-rounded women are waiting for me.

My maids, apparently.

I've never needed one. Why would I need six?

"We drew a bath for you, and then we will head to the springs," one of the oldest ones says.

A bath? When was the last time I had one of those? And what does she mean by springs?

I sulk to the tub and flick my hand through the water. Warm. But they're all still here, staring at me. There's been way too much staring in my direction today. How idiotic of me, to think I wanted to be noticed for once.

A couple of the women hold vases. Another holds a brush, and yet another holds a tray of what I think are soaps. I've never seen such tiny, elegant, colored soaps before. What's the purpose behind everything I've been through and what they want me to go through?

"I will do this myself," I say.

As one, they nod—who trained these people?—and set their things down on a table by the bath. They file out of the room, except for the one who spoke before.

She says, "We will return in half an hour if that suits you."

"It does," I reply. I'll have this done in ten.

As soon as she closes the door behind her, I strip, grateful to get out of these sweat-crusted clothes, and get in the tub. The water feels good on my aching body. I grab a soap bar at random and a scrub brush and run them across my hands as if the past will go with the layers of skin if I scour hard enough.

It doesn't.

Ten minutes later, I'm clean and dressed. I explore the room, checking every nook and cranny. Every drawer and under the bed. The drawers are carved with intricacy. The four-poster bed is sumptuously soft. I wouldn't be able to sleep on such a thing. Even the carpet is more cushioned than my bed back at Daros's. The curtains are a red velvet that matches the drapes around the bed.

As far as I can tell, this place is unoccupied. There are no personal belongings. Might as well be my room at Daros's house if it wasn't so refined and furnished.

Twenty minutes later, the women return. The one who spoke before glances at me, her cheeks pulled down in a perpetual scowl. She's tall, easily the tallest one here, and thick boned. Her eyes are small on her face, while concentrating heavily on me. For a moment, I think she disapproves of the job I did. If she doesn't like how I clean myself, she'll have to get over that aversion quickly.

"Please follow me, Your Highness," she says.

Not as bad as *Your Majesty*, but still not right. What do I want to be called? I don't know. Something not so... pretentious.

I haven't thought much about not having a name. Once, when I was still small, I asked Daros why I didn't have one. His response was that I didn't deserve one. Calling me *girl* was good enough for him. It should still be good enough for what I am.

I deserve nothing more.

The woman leads me through the palace via a different route than the one I followed before, her steps in time to some rhythm I can't hear or follow. The area isn't unlike before, despite going all this way—drapes around huge windows; portraits of unfamiliar people or landscapes on the walls; and flowers here and there, on tables dotting the halls, in pots, or in corners. Beauty the likes of which I know of and have seen but haven't owned.

The maid opens a door that leads to a muggy room, outside of which wait several guards, male and female, dressed in steel and black. The room is large, with a pool of smooth marble in the middle and pillars on the sides. Everything is white and pure in here.

Everything except me. I'm anything but pure.

"This is the queen's bathing room," the woman says.

"I already took a bath."

She lifts a brow. "That was to prepare you for this experience. May I please assist you?"

I'd rather cut off my own finger.

She gets the message because she points at the vials and combs next to the pool and says, "Here are your bathing necessities."

There are more items here than I've ever owned at one time. Not that it's something I'd tell her. Instead, I try to hide my surprise. "What are they all for?"

"Are you certain you don't want assistance?" she asks instead of answering.

I add an edge to my voice. "What are they all for?"

She inches back.

Good. She knows who she's dealing with.

She explains the items one at a time and slowly, but it's still more than I can handle. A soap with grit, to make my skin smooth. One to make me shine. One to make me smell like a queen. Why do I need a soap for that? And why does the queen have to smell a certain way?

She shows me fat-toothed combs to get out tangles. A strange-looking tool to massage the scalp. A brush. And more items that blur together. How am I going to remember all this?

Doesn't matter. No one needs this much for just a bath, let alone life. If it was something important like poison, I would remember every word she spoke.

Once she stops droning on, I tell her to leave, and she does so. I get a better look around the room. So many pillars around this place. Too many places to hide.

I burst into a run around the pillars, boots smacking against the marble. I quiet my steps as I go and check each place someone could hide behind. I can't imagine the palace people would leave someone in here with the Queen when I clearly want to be alone, but then again, minutes ago I couldn't dream that anyone took two baths in a row. Especially in a pool of such elegance.

There's no one behind any of the pillars, and though the room is large, I'm not even breathing hard by the time I return.

Good. I'm still at my best.

The only door is the one I came through, and it's shut. I should have privacy. Not that I trust it. One never knows where there are peepholes or secret entrances.

I hurry into the pool, the water sluicing across me. It's more perfect than the bathwater, somehow smoother than normal.

While the water waves around me, I wonder about the Mortum Tura. How does the cup choose the next queen? What does it look for in a queen? It can't be by anything good—virtue, kindness, or purity of heart—because I'm an assassin.

Does it matter? Maybe it's all random. I brush it aside. Despite my misgivings, I find myself luxuriating in too many of the items. Not that I know what they're all for. The smell of roses makes me feel almost carefree.

I take my time scrubbing even though I already feel clean. I even get between my toes, the mole between my big toe and the one next to it on my right foot stubbornly holding on. No other spots mar my body but that one. Daros was careful not to do any lasting damage.

Once I'm done—or rather, once I've gone overboard—I hurriedly rinse in the pool. I get out, dry off, and dress as quickly as possible in the garment left for me. It's a flimsy thing—a thin layer of material which covers me, though it's big. A dress. Something I don't wear. Another thing I have to remedy.

A faint patter behind me is the only warning I get before a rope digs into my neck and my back smashes against someone behind me. Someone big and strong. It has to be a man, the way he's gripping me. If I wasn't so busy choking, I'd smile. This is what I wanted, only not in the way I expected.

Why this person wants me dead, I'll never know, but he's doing me quite the favor.

My instincts peak to life. Not a lot, but enough to make my

reflexes flare. I lean forward, then head-butt the man and connect with his neck. He sputters and jerks backward but instead of letting go, he takes me with him.

My vision flickers. Where are my daggers when I need them?

That decides it. I still deserve to die, but it will be on my terms, not this brute's.

I press his trigger points on his wrist, and immediately, icy air cools my neck with the rope's release. I duck, jabbing my elbows back as I go. There's an *umpf* behind me. I somersault forward, then spin to face my opponent.

His face is an unfamiliar mix of pox marks and sheen. He grunts and comes at me head on, rope still in hand. Guilt sluices through me, but he did bring the attack to me.

I spin out of the way at the last moment, hitting his kidney as he passes by. His faint cry brings the sound of footsteps hurrying through the hall toward us.

The look on his face says he knows we'll soon no longer be alone. A meaty hand grabs my arm before I can slip away. I kick him where it will hurt the most before he can dodge out of the way. He lets go with a grunt. It was low of me, but I don't want to be under his thumb when help arrives.

I kick his groaning self into the pool. As he goes in with a splash, others enter the room.

That was not nearly quick enough of them. Where did the assassin come from, and why did he want to take my life? Is he one of Daros's men? Someone I don't know? Did Daros already find me, or is someone else after my life now that I'm the queen, even though it's been a scant time?

"You might want to be faster next time," I tell the two men and the tall woman staring at me with wide eyes, frozen in their places. And then I leave the way I came.

My hands tremble something fierce.

Why didn't I let him finish me off?

CHAPTER 4

GUARDS SWARM AROUND ME. I can't help but wonder where they were when my life was threatened. The would-be assassin is dragged off by another group of soldiers, all of whom are soaking wet. I want to question him. To find out where he came from. Who he's working for. But I don't know how to go about it; torturing people for information was always Daros's job.

I have to know, though. Before I realize what I'm doing, I call out, "Bring him here."

Ranen is immediately by my side. I didn't know he was around. "Your Majesty, let someone else take care of this, and we can inform you of what we find out. It would be beneath you to speak with the prisoner."

I want to let go. To take back my words. But I don't need another Daros in my life, bossing me around, even if I plan on not being around long. I glare at Ranen. I stood up once; I can do it again.

My jaw wants to clamp shut. Instead, I force out, "That doesn't matter."

"Your Highness, I must protest. It isn't safe."

That matters even less. "I will talk to him. Now."

JANEAL FALOR

The tassel on Ranen's hat dips down as he bows, but the gesture is stiff. Jerky. "Yes, My Lady."

He motions the guards to bring the prisoner closer. A woman holds one arm while a man holds the other. I ignore him in favor of the would-be assassin. I take in more of him than when he was trying to kill me—his ragged hair, burnt nose, and cool eyes. The eyes of a killer.

Do mine look like that?

I swallow past my tight throat. "Who sent you?"

His cool gaze searches my eyes. He sneers. "You may be the queen, but I don't answer to you."

I press my knuckles against his temple, middle finger still curled but jutted out. "You can, and you will. If not, I can make you perish."

He has the audacity to laugh—a cruel, vain sound. He clenches a muscle in his jaw, and then he spits on my face.

Without a thought, I slug him as hard as I can. He grunts, head jerking back. I wipe the spittle off my face, and try not to grimace in disgust as I swipe it across the cloth on his shoulder. It's not the worst I've faced.

Everyone around us is silent. Watching. Waiting.

Why don't they do something more to protect me? To honor me? Not that I deserve it, but I am their sovereign now.

I jab my fingers behind the prisoner's collarbone and force him to the ground. "Who sent you?"

He winces but clamps his mouth shut.

I grit my teeth, pushing harder. Still, he doesn't reply.

"You've done enough questioning, Your Majesty," Ranen barks out.

I release the prisoner, wishing I hadn't stooped to Daros's level. What's more, I wish others weren't here to see it. My face burns at the thought that I'm anything like him—a cruel, unfeeling person. But I am.

Nothing could be plainer.

"Take him to the dungeons," Ranen says.

The guards lift the prisoner off the ground and drag him away. Now it's Ranen, the servant who showed me the baths, and me.

Ranen glares at me. I glance at the ground. Heat burns within me. I want to tell him off, but what if his rebuttals are anything like Daros's?

I can handle it. Besides, I doubt Ranen has the stomach for real torture. I lift my chin.

"What will happen to him now?" I put bite behind my words.

"Your Majesty, I must insist you not trouble yourself with such things. It's unbecoming, and I won't put up with it." He waves a finger at me, like I'm an errant child.

I bristle. He won't put up with it? What about what I want?

But then I remember what brought me here. He might not be punishing me like Daros would, but that doesn't mean I have the right to voice my thoughts.

That is, until I spot the servant. I turn my attention to her, not caring about Ranen. "How did the prisoner slip past you?"

"I don't know, Your Highness." Her gaze is focused on the ground. "I will take whatever punishment you see fit for letting him through."

I contemplate what to do. "What about the two men who entered with you? Did they notice him enter?"

"They saw nothing either. They are now with the guards, taking the prisoner to the dungeons. But I promise you we had nothing to do with it. We would give our lives for you. Otherwise we wouldn't be here. Perhaps he used a secret entrance. There are many hidden tunnels throughout the palace."

Ranen glares at her. "I see," I say. And I do. More than I would like. I've gone after others' lives many times, after all.

It seems I'll have to watch myself closely if I value my life. Which I don't. Do I?

"We should call for more guards to protect her," the servant says to Ranen.

"Very well. Run and fetch someone." His tone is clipped.

"I would, but I have to help Her Majesty get into proper attire and fix her hair, so she is fit to be seen."

Seeing how I'm in a dress, it's not possible. I've carried off dresses before, though, so I can do it again until I decide what to do with my life if I have to.

Ranen flares his nostrils the tiniest bit, but I catch on. He's upset. Because he has to leave my side? Because my life was threatened? Or because he doesn't want me to be alone with the servant? What is he worried about?

"Very well." He storms off.

I don't bother telling the servant I don't need a guard. It's true, but there's no point.

"Now, let's get your dress on properly and your hair fixed," the servant says.

Letting numbness creep over me, I follow her back to my rooms. The vanity now holds lots of combs, brushes, and vials. I sit in the chair in front of the mirror, grateful I can see the servant in it.

One thing I know—I don't trust either her or Ranen.

I avoid looking my image in the eye as the tall woman does my hair up, digging pins into my scalp. Somehow she manages to put my hair up, despite it being so short.

My dark-brown hair, the color of many others in this country, is thick. My face is round, but not with fat. Not like all of the Kurah class—those rich enough to glut themselves. No, my cheeks are sunken in. My lips are full but pale, and the eyes I can no longer avoid…

Haunted.

Their blue depths are startling with their loss of humanity.

I look away, unable to bear the sight.

Once finished with my hair, my servant helps me into a gown that's the silkiest thing I've ever touched—so smooth and sleek. But far too beautiful. Plus, she has to pin it many times to get it to fit on me.

She paints my face with what feels like a heavy hand, but I don't want to look in the mirror again to find out. There's only so much I can take.

"There," she says. "You're ready for the day. You'll spend most of it with Ranen."

I force myself not to cringe.

"If you'll excuse me, Your Majesty, I must see to a few things." She curtsies. "Ranen will be here with your bodyguards soon, if they aren't already."

She leaves the room, and I allow myself to relax the slightest bit. I miss my old room, back at Daros's. Didn't think that would be true, but it is.

Pushing the thought aside, I move to where I stashed my blades and pouch earlier. I don't know what I was thinking, going without them.

Well, perhaps I do. Perhaps I wanted the opportunity to lose my life. A queen is never safe.

I grab them now, though. Without them, I was naked. I need my blades more than I need food. I even rip a hole in one of my pockets, to accommodate one of them. They're probably meant for embroidery, but this is a better purpose. It doesn't matter if the dress is destroyed. There are much more important things than frivolous clothes.

CHAPTER 5

THE THOUGHT of wanting to preserve my life still haunts me as the day wears on. I've nibbled on some food—nothing much but enough to alleviate my hunger pains—and Ranen is jabbering on over topics I couldn't care less about while we sit in an unfamiliar room.

The room has more landscapes of Valcora on the walls, a clock, no windows, and two bodyguards posted on either side of the door, both women. More are waiting outside, a mixture of genders. There's a long table surrounded by chairs, but the only two seats occupied are mine and—across from me—Ranen's. And he's still talking.

None of it seems to have anything to do with being queen. More like bossing me around. Stuff about how to sit, what utensils to use when eating, and how to give a proper curtsy. He says I'm to let him take care of the nitty-gritty, boring things, while I focus on putting up a good front.

I think on my almost-death and why I didn't let myself die. Instinct, I guess. Nothing else can account for it.

If only if I didn't have a death wish, then I would still be on the streets alone instead of listening to this moron prattle on. Of course, I'd be cold and hungry, but I'd also be by myself.

He's saying something about dancing now. Knives forbid he makes me practice. If he tries, I'll pull out the daggers I stashed on my person. I won't be going anywhere without them again. I shouldn't have gone without them in the first place, I know better than that. But then, it's hard to care when all you want is to no longer be around.

Maybe if I can find out who wanted me dead, I'll feel free to die. It's a hard question. I don't know who to suspect, so I suspect everyone.

A group of frilly and refined girls enters the room. Some sulk, others glare, and two are expressionless.

Some are familiar. Why?

I place one then. A blur of a memory, but it's enough. These are the girls I burst through when I made my dive for the Mortum Tura.

What are they doing here? Could any of them have something to do with the assassination attempt? I doubt they are all innocent. No one is without mistakes. I learned that while bloodying my hands, if nothing else.

"You'll need to thank each one of them," Ranen says.

"Who are they, and why do they need to be thanked?" Daros taught me not to be grateful for anything. Ever.

"They are those who trained to become queen. Those who went the proper way about it." His tone holds a blade of reprimand.

Like I care about proper ways of things, except the upkeep of lifesaving tools. "Why didn't they drink it before me, then?"

"Because you shoved your way in." His blunt manner would take me aback if I wasn't used to it from Daros. I thought as queen I would have less of that, but perhaps things are different than I expected.

Another question finds its way to my lips. "Why didn't they take it in the weeks before I came?"

"Because, Your Majesty"—more like *nitwit*, by his tone—"they weren't prepared until this day."

Apparently, neither was I. "Why do I need to thank them?"

"For their service, of course." His voice implies that any idiot could figure that out.

It doesn't make sense to me, but I'm used to following orders.

As the women come nearer, they don't look all that happy to see me. If they went the proper way to becoming queen, and I came along and took it, they have a right to be angry.

As each one comes forward, I thank them, though I still have no idea what I'm thanking them for.

It's the last girl's turn, and her eyes flare like she wants to take me out this very moment.

I'd like to see her try.

She's short and well rounded. They all are chubby. Must have been well fed, getting trained to become queen. She has a dainty mole above her lip and to the right. I bet she thinks it's beautiful and becoming. Who knows? It may even be fake.

"These women will become your ladies in waiting," Ranen says.

"My what?"

He clenches his jaw. "Your ladies in waiting. They will attend you at functions. Keep you company. Run errands for you. Things of that nature."

"I see." I don't really. Those are things I either don't need or can do myself. Why would I have someone else do them for me? "Why them?"

He gives an exasperated sigh. "Because they trained the right way. Not to possibly become queen, but also to serve her, should the chance arise before they die or become royalty themselves."

Does that mean I saved some of their lives? They didn't get the chance to drink. Never tasted the sweet bitterness of the Mortum Tura. Then again, maybe I stopped the next girl who was going to drink it from becoming queen.

No wonder some are glaring daggers at me. I hope the few who didn't want to die, who unlike me, are thankful, though. "And this is how it's always done?" I ask.

"It is." An unspoken *and you will respect it* hangs in the air.

It's all a bunch of hooey. Still, I hurry and thank them to get

Ranen off my back. Anything to get rid of him faster. The women don't seem to care about my *thank yous*, though. I'd be better off not opening my mouth at all.

"I will leave you now so you can get to know your ladies-in-waiting, but don't forget what I have taught you so far. You will have more lessons tomorrow, but now I have better things to do."

More lessons? How long am I going to have to sit and listen to their petty concerns? I should have picked a different way of death. Or just let the man kill me.

Ranen leaves the room, and all that's left are these thirteen girls and women who look as if being in my presence is torture. They know nothing about pain.

Most look to be about my age or a little older. Some are middle-aged, and one woman appears grandmotherly. They all look prim and proper, despite being angry at my presence.

The girl with the mole asks, "Why did you drink from the cup?"

I narrow my eyes at her. "What is your name?"

"Jem," she says with a curtsy, then spits out, "Your Majesty."

"Well, Jem"—I say her name as sarcastically as I can; if she can be rude, I can certainly dish it back—"why did you want to drink from the cup?"

She scoffs. "As if you have to ask."

"Exactly my point." Which is all they're getting from me on the subject. There's no way I'm telling them more.

"I heard you staved off an attacker," says the grandmotherly woman. Why she wanted to be queen is beyond me. She has so many wrinkles, her time as the ruler would be short—if she made it in the first place. Now I suppose she won't know. It's just as well for her.

"And your name is…?" I ask

"Faya."

"Well then, Faya, yes. Someone attacked me." I glance at Jem. "Anyone who attacks me is dealt with accordingly."

The room grows quiet after that, as if no one dares speak.

The ladies pull out things to work on, like little sewing pieces

JANEAL FALOR

stashed in their voluminous skirts. If I pull out what's stashed in my skirts, some of them will faint on the spot. Like my daggers.

"Excuse me, Your Majesty," Faya says. "We would like to know where we can find your family, to move them into the palace."

"Why would you want to do such a thing?" The closest thing I have to family is Daros, and having him here is not going to happen.

"It is one of our duties, as ladies-in-waiting."

"Well, it is one duty you won't have to worry about."

Jem narrows her eyes, and a few others look on curiously, but none of them contradict my words.

"What about your name?" Faya asks. "What can we call you, My Lady?"

"It seems you have plenty of names for me as it is." I don't want to admit to being nameless. I've never wanted to before, and I feel even less inclined to now.

"Forgive me, Your Majesty, but we need to call you *Queen Something*. What can we fill that in with?" Faya persists.

"Nothing. You will call me only *Queen*." I put sufficient bite in my words that the ladies-in-waiting shouldn't ask more questions.

And they don't, but they do give each other bewildered glances. It's not like people such as me exist. Everyone has a name, unless they belong to Daros, and I'm the only one who belongs to him.

They continue sewing. It makes me want to pull out those daggers to gouge my own eyes out. I can't handle this boring busywork.

A while later, I've had enough. There's only so much sitting around a person can do. It doesn't matter that I was taught to emulate those around me. There's no reason to, and I'm more bored than a knife can be dull.

I stand, and the ladies hurry to their feet, putting away their sewing.

"Is there something you need?" the oldest one, Faya, asks.

"Yes. Take me to my room."

"I wish I could, my lady, but it's almost time for the feast to begin."'

"What feast?"

"The one in honor of you becoming queen. Lord Ranen should have told you all about it and what to expect. It's always held the afternoon after a new leader is chosen."

Either he didn't, or I was paying less attention than I thought. "When should I attend this feast?"

She glances at the clock. "In another twenty or so minutes."

I clamp my teeth together and sit back down. This is ridiculous. I thought I'd left my mandates behind, but it seems not. Even as queen, you're subject to others.

We wait, them doing their handwork and fussing over me for what seems more like forty minutes before Jem stands. The others follow suit, Faya more slowly than the others. At this point, I'm so grumpy of doing nothing at all that I stay in my seat to be contrary.

"It's time for us to go, Your Majesty," Jem says.

"I'll go when I'm good and ready."

Jem gives me a shocked look, like she doesn't believe what I said. The others look just as horrified.

"You can't do that," one of them says. "We have to be on time."

"I'm the queen. I can do whatever I want." And if they're going to bore me for hours, I can make them wait for me. I couldn't pull such a ploy with Daros. Being able to do so now has me hiding a smirk.

I sit here, casually thinking of the best poison to use on annoying twits. There are so many wondrous options. Not that I would really do it to such innocents, but it's entertaining to think on.

They all stare at me, aghast. I haven't enjoyed myself this much in a long time. Maybe having to sit here for hours, doing nothing, was worth it. Fifteen minutes later, I stand. The others look relieved and lead me to the door.

As we make our way to the feast, I can't help but think I may figure out a way to fit in here. Until I find out who sent the assassin, that is. After that, I will see if I choose life or death.

CHAPTER 6

My earliest memory is of being on the street.

Cold.

Hungry.

Alone.

Strangely enough, that's how I feel now, though I shouldn't. The room's the perfect temperature, and I sit in front of a table full of food, surrounded by people. There's food to feast on for weeks, and I get sick looking at it, knowing how starving I was yesterday. It's all here, nonetheless—a celebration in my honor.

But there's nothing to celebrate. My plate is filled for me, my glass kept full, yet all I can do is sip and remember those days on the streets. I was mostly numb, but there were times when I badly wanted something like this. And now that I have it, I no longer want it.

Don't deserve it.

I pick at my food, hunger forcing me to eat but despair making it dry within my mouth.

Jem and the other ladies in waiting are close by, along with Ranen. This is the most uncomfortable meal I've ever lived through, and I've lived through some very uncomfortable meals, with Daros threatening people and once going further than a threat. Eating on the floor as punishment when I did something wrong was preferable to being at his eye level and risking his wrath.

At least no one here tries to talk to me. For having a party in my honor, they don't seem to care about me.

Everyone here appears to be part of the Kurah class—fine clothing, fancy hair, makeup for the girls. It's all a little over the top. Lots of gold and jewels being flaunted about. Where are the rest of the people I'm supposed to be queen of? Or is this some sort of show for the cream of society?

"Your Highness." A servant bows low, holding a serving tray out toward me with one hand. On it sits the very same chalice I drank from and became queen.

I grab it, eager for its contents. If I drink from it again, the spell may be undone. I may die like I was supposed to. Like I couldn't let myself before.

I lift the cup to my lips.

"Your Highness," the screechy man sitting next to me says, "if I may be so bold, you are to give a speech before drinking."

A speech? What in all of Valcora would I say? There are no words left inside me. Nothing left but a tumble of emotions I can't deal with. Guilt stings me with the blood, cold on my hands. Hatred toward myself and the daggers and poisons I use. Shame for ever listening to Daros.

Forget protocol.

I chug down the contents of the cup without a single word. The room is silent. Some of the liquid spills out and rolls down my chin. As soon as the drink is gone, I slam my cup down, waiting for pain.

Of course, just like before, it doesn't come. Instead, something tickles at me. It's almost like the thread of a memory, but I can't imagine what type of memory it could be. It's not familiar.

The crowd watches me with a mixture of confusion and disgust as I grab a linen napkin and wipe the spill on my chin. When they continue to stare at me and do nothing, I say in my loudest voice, "I am the queen."

I stand, and the entire group stands as well. They bow low to the ground. What is with these people and bowing? I stride away from the room, putting as much anger as I can in each step. This was the worst possible feast I could attend.

I don't stop when I pass the guards. Don't stop when I get to the hall. Don't stop even when I lose my way. I stretch my legs, my skirts rustling as I go. Footsteps follow me, but I ignore them. I'm not going to have a moment to myself as queen, it would seem.

I try to outrun the feelings jumbled in my chest. My eyes sting in an unfamiliar way. The thing that finally makes me come to a halt is a dead end. I slouch against the wall and rest my forehead on the cool stone, wishing it would fall atop me.

Why do I never have good ideas?

It would be better if I gave a speech. If only I wasn't so eager to drink from the cup that made me queen. I should have known it wouldn't kill me. That I'm stuck in this position.

Why did it choose me? Why couldn't it have chosen one of those other girls, like Jem or Faya, after it killed me off? A burning desire to understand fills me, but as far as I'm aware, no one knows how the cup works.

When I turn around, heat sears my face. A guard is watching me. I knew he was here, but I didn't expect him to be staring at me.

He's young, though a couple years older than my seventeenish years, I think. He's several inches taller than me, with brown hair several inches long. He's strong, evident by the muscles where his shirt doesn't cover, though his armor prevents me from seeing much. His armor is like everyone else's of the guard. A light steel vest with black breeches, high black boots, and a black cape so they can blend in if needed. He has a sword on one side and a couple knives strapped to the other.

Mostly, it's his eyes that capture me. They're hazel, with hints of blue. He lowers his gaze making me miss the view. "Forgive me, Your Majesty. I didn't mean to intrude. I'm to keep you safe."

A heavy sigh escapes me. There's one benefit to this. No longer being lost, though I'd almost rather stay here at this cool, dead end. Almost. "Would you please take me to my room?"

He gives a short bow. "Of course." He turns and walks away, though he looks over his shoulder every once and a while.

I move next to him, though I'm in no hurry to do so. We wind through more hallways than I've seen in all my life. I suppose I saw them on the way out, but I was too angry to really see them.

When we've been walking a full minute or so, the guard slows. I linger behind him, but he doesn't continue on. He faces me, gaze still lowered. "It's not my place to say anything—I know I could be put to death for it—but I want to know. Why would you risk your life to become queen?"

I can't help the smile that tilts up one side of my face. Finally someone here who's not a coward or rude. "What's your name?"

"Nash. What is yours, my queen?"

"I have no name."

He widens his eyes, and his mouth tilts open.

I clench my jaw. "Show me the way to my room."

He bows yet again and moves forward, like he didn't ask the question to begin with. There's no apology in his movements. No sorrow in his steps. We pass other people, who bow as I walk by. I ignore them.

When we reach what I believe to be my rooms, Ranen is waiting for me with a retinue. I grit my teeth. I'm already sick of him.

"My lady," he says, "we were worried about you. Especially after the attack. You need to stay where we can find you."

I open my mouth to explain myself, but then realize if there's anything good about being queen, it's that I don't have to explain myself any longer. "Leave."

"My lady?"

I turn to the other admirers, still bowing to me. "All of you, leave now."

They stare at me, aghast. They'd better get used to it. As a matter of fact, I'd better get used to it.

"Except you." I point to the guard who helped me find this room, who is turning away. "You come with me."

Without watching to see if they will obey or not, I turn the knob on my door and hurry through. The guard, thankfully, follows.

"Shut the door," I tell him.

Once he does so, I take the time to look around the first room. I was here earlier, when I bathed and dressed, but I passed through the sitting room quickly and didn't stop to look at the details, of which there are many.

It's a big room—much bigger than my bedroom at Daros's—and gaudy, with gold clinging to every place I look. Real gold, if I had to guess, taken from one of the man mines in Valcora. Cluttered with the furniture as it is, it holds no appeal. The chairs and sofas look more uncomfortable than a torture device, and I know my torture devices. I wince and focus on the walls. Landscape paintings are all there is, besides a window.

I huff and move to the bedroom. The guard doesn't follow. Smart man. I kick off my shoes and climb on the high bed. Once I'm situated and certain my skirts maintain my modesty do I call him in. Not that I care, but I find myself wanting to make an impression on the only person who's spoken to me like I'm real.

He enters, showing no hint of discomfort at being called into the queen's very own bedroom.

"Sit," I say.

To my astonishment, he leaves the room. I'm befuddled until he walks back in with one of those horrid chairs.

"You're not going to sit in that, are you?" I scowl.

He lifts an eyebrow, places the chair directly across from me, and sits.

"Well, well, well… you've certainly proven you don't care for comfort."

"I care for propriety."

I can't help myself. "And yet, here you are, in my bedroom."

"Only because you care for comfort."

Huh. "Tell me about how things work here."

"That's a lot to cover."

"It's what I need to know." I pause and then add, "From someone other than Ranen."

"What? You don't like him?"

I snort.

"That's very queenly of you," he says.

"I try." I attempt not to squirm. "Now, what do I need to know?"

CHAPTER 7

"WHAT HAVE YOU LEARNED THIS FAR?" Nash asks, sitting closer to the door than to me.

My face heats. I turn toward my window so he won't notice. "Um... nothing."

The room fills with silence.

"They haven't taught you anything yet?" He sighs.

"Well, they tried, but I wasn't paying attention." The admission costs me more than I want to admit. Could it be that I care what he thinks of me even more than I thought? I can't imagine why.

"Are you sure you want me to be the one to teach you? There are people who know the protocols better than me."

I shrug, turning to face him again. "Protocol doesn't concern me. I want something useful. Tell me—what do you know of the secret tunnels in this place?"

"You're going to have to learn it one way or another. It can't be ignored."

"And you can't ignore my question. Secret tunnels?"

He shakes his head before moving closer. "Those exist, but I know of only the well-used one the guards use to get from place to place or to intercept threats to those living here."

"Are there threats often?"

He gives me a level glance. "You've already been threatened. It will continue to happen."

So much for knowing who was behind the assassination attempt. If such attempts are frequent, it's a matter of time before another happens. I must figure out if I want to live before the next one. This way, I'll be prepared to choose—death or fighting.

"Why are there so many threats?" I suspect several things. Mostly people who either want to be queen or want the queen as their puppet.

Though spoken with care, his words confirm this. "You have a highly sought position. All it takes for it to be open again is your demise."

"Do you know who sent the man that's now in the dungeons after me?"

"I regret to say I do not. Isn't Lord Ranen trying to find out?"

I shrug. "He said he would, but I haven't heard any word on it. Doubt that he's trying very hard, but it's possible."

"I can ask around—see what the guards know. But don't be surprised if I come back with nothing."

That's generous of him. More so than I'd expect. "Let me know if you discover anything." Apparently, I still care about my life.

"I will."

I contemplate asking for the secret tunnel he's familiar with, but it's of no use to me if it's frequented often. What else do I need to know? I'm somewhat familiar with parts of the palace, but it's so huge, it's difficult to perceive it all. I got lost in it moments ago. "Can you draw me a map of this place?" I ask.

"I can do one better. I'll ask a servant to bring us the plans we have. They aren't comprehensive, but they are a good place to start."

"How does a guard learn about these plans?"

"I studied them in an effort to understand the best ways to move around. I serve the queen and therefore need to know about the things surrounding her that concern her possible safety." He stands. "If you'll excuse me, I'll send for them."

He leaves and closes the door behind him.

I focus on the window. It's like the one back at Daros's. A nice view, but so small it highlights my captivity. Because I feel like a captive, even as the queen. Like the last one, this window too is barely large enough for me to climb out of, which will come in handy.

The door opens, and Nash resumes his seat. "It will be here as soon as they can fetch it."

And in the meantime, what? It's not the first time I've encountered silence. Daros used it to great effect. It had a better result when I was younger, though. Now I'm accustomed to it.

Nash apparently doesn't feel the same way. "What else would you like to learn about?"

I purse my lips and tap a finger to them. "What do you know of the other guards?"

"Some are loyal to the crown. Some are loyal to one person or another."

"Which group do you belong to?" Not that I expect an honest answer.

"The crown, though I know it's hard to believe. My parents raised me right. Taught me honor and respect. My loyalty is now meant for you."

His words stir something to life. What, I can't be sure. "It's true, I have a hard time believing it, but I hope you prove me wrong. Which guards can be trusted?"

"Afet, Stird, and Wilric are all loyal. I'd stake my life on it. Eldim may or may not be. It's hard to tell with him."

So few? I can't be surprised with what I know, but it remains a bit of a shock. "How do you know they're loyal?"

"They almost gave their lives for the last queen," he says. "A man broke into the palace. It happens on occasion. Be prepared for it. He was wielding a sword and hacking at anyone who got in his way. Afet, Stird, and Wilric ran toward him when he neared the queen, while the rest ran away. All three sustained injuries but have since recovered. The last queen gave them gold as a reward, but they remained here, doing their duty."

That's compelling. "You believe that loyalty extends to me?"

"I do."

"And Eldim?"

"He has a habit of not listening to those who would sway him away from the crown, but I haven't seen him do anything to defend the queen to a degree that would imply absolute loyalty."

That's something to think about.

A knock on the sitting room door draws my attention.

Nash answers it. After a moment, he comes back in the room with several large papers in hand. "These are the maps of the palace."

"There are so many." I don't know what I expected, but not this. The print is tiny and the paper so gigantic, it's hard to imagine anything being of that size.

"The palace has been added onto over the years. Many rulers wanted to make it bigger. Give of herself to the building, in some way."

He moves to the side of the bed, and I follow.

He spreads the papers across the mattress. "The palace, for your perusal. I imagine it will take weeks before it's committed to your memory, but this here"—he points to a few squares halfway down the page and to the right—"are your rooms. If you start here and work outward, you'll get it in time." He draws a line toward a large rectangle. "This room is where the Mortum Tura is taken." He moves to a slightly smaller rectangle, not far off. "And this is where most of your interactions will take place. The government uses this room most often. The other pages are different floors of the palace, should you need to use one of the upper rooms."

"More rooms than anyone needs, just on this one floor."

"Rightly so, but they are here all the same. Do you think you'll have a problem transferring the map to the real world?"

"None." He'll be surprised by how quickly I pick things up. I'm a fast learner.

We pore over the map. Despite this, it feels like there's so much I need to know, yet so little I care about.

When I let out a yawn, I know it's past usefulness's time. "You will come back in the morning and tell me more."

"Yes, Your Majesty."

"You're promoted to Head"—I wave my hand around like a dunce—"*Whatever.*"

"*Head Whatever*. Everyone will look up to me."

My lips twitch. "What position would you suggest?"

"I don't need a position to help you, but you will have to release me from the army. While I can protect you when I'm here, I also hold duties that are beyond you."

"I want you to have a position anyway. Ranen is the Head Advisor. That's your new title."

"I'm just a simple guard."

"Not anymore."

He stands, getting out of that chair that has to be really uncomfortable. "At least I can offer you protection while I'm at your side."

"I don't need protection."

"That much is evident from what I heard about you taking down the would-be assassin. Still, it doesn't hurt to have someone else watching your back."

I wonder what that would be like—to have someone I can truly trust help keep me safe. It's not something I can fathom. Besides, no matter what Nash says, there's no way I can trust him. There's no one I can trust, except myself.

CHAPTER 8

DESPITE BEING TIRED, I can't sleep. It's just as well; nightmares are not welcome. Images of things I've done come back to haunt me with glaring cruelty when I sleep. Blood, daggers, poison—it's all there, always waiting for me to try to rest so they can torment me.

I wish there were pants in my new drawers besides a whole lot of nothing. The ones I wore when I came in have disappeared. Not caring about the material of the outfit I'm wearing, I strip down to the flimsy dress I had on earlier.

When it's all I have on, I pull out a blade and cut off the skirt just above the knees. The material drops to the carpet. I slice the sides of the skirt for maneuverability. Once ready, I slip to my window. The white wall outside that goes around the entire palace grounds is teaming with soldiers. They're all facing outward, though. No one is looking toward my rooms. They probably think the outside wall of the palace is unscaleable, but there are enough juts in the stone to make it work. I sneak out my window and scurry up the wall.

I pass by several windows, one of which has a light in. I peek inside to find Ranen, drinking and writing something down. I wonder what notes he's making, but I don't stick around to find out. The rest of the rooms are empty or their occupants have gone to bed.

I keep climbing until I get to the roof, where I begin wandering around. It's a familiar movement, even if this roof is huger. I used to escape to the roof after a beating from Daros. Well, one of his men he hired out. He wouldn't dirty his hands with a beating. He would do other things, though. Torture me with hot oil or shove me underwater until I thought I was going to die. Choking was one of his favorite things to do to me.

The memories are too strong. They have me curling into a ball with only my eyes sticking out over my knees. My stomach roils. It's true he wouldn't torture me often during the last few years. Had to keep me in my prime, he said. But that didn't mean it never happened anymore. It was at least a weekly occurrence. I couldn't ever seem to behave as he wanted me to.

I'm trembling, and not from the cold. I hold myself together more tightly, trying to force away the thoughts. Evil exists and isn't hard to find at all. Everyone seems to be full of it. No one ever had a problem beating me for Daros. No one offered true care or sympathy.

Not until I saw her eyes.

I force several blinks as tears come, and I think on something else. I was trained to do one thing I didn't want to do. Why did I have to be abandoned by my parents? Why did Daros have to be the one to take me in?

I never understood. Never will.

I drag my gaze across the landscape before me, hoping to find release from my thoughts. From the roof, the city of Indell looks almost alive. The capitol rarely sleeps. Lights flicker like twinkling stars, as far as I can see. The city goes on and on. How am I over not only this city but a whole country? I don't know, but it's beautiful.

But beauty is ice, crystalline at first but melting easily.

Three of the five moons shine down on me, the red-tinted one in the middle and the white ones on each side. They seem to know something I don't. I'm sure they've seen more of this country than I ever will. What's more, they've seen foreign lands. How different would my life be if my parents abandoned me in another country, away from Daros?

Did any previous queens find themselves up here, staring down at the country they ruled? If they did, I bet they didn't get here by climbing.

I wish I had the chance to talk to one of them, so they could give me some idea what to expect. Words from a woman who actually ruled, not a pompous guy who believes he should be ruling instead.

How am I supposed to do this job? Even with Nash's help, it's like I'm lost in the mountains, surrounded by carnivorous animals. It's not been a full day yet. This is ridiculous and impossible. Why did I have to pick a way to die that would lead to more trouble than I've ever had?

Do I want my life? I don't think I do, but things feel different now. I'm not sure how, but the gnawing ache inside my chest isn't as painful.

I scout out the roof until I'm bone weary. I'll explore farther tomorrow. For now, I climb back down to my room, change into a nightdress, and plop onto the bed.

Even if sleep is long in coming, I'm done thinking on things I can do nothing about. I clear my mind and wait for morning.

CHAPTER 9

As I LIE in bed with my eyes closed, the night flickers with images I can't quite place. I try to bring one into focus, but it stays blurry and far gone. I push and pull at it, doing whatever I can to make it come closer. To see what or who is invading my dreams.

But nothing happens.

I sit up, leaning against my headboard, ready to wait it out until morning. It shouldn't be long now, and at least it's not a nightmare. Just a fuzz of something I should know, but I can't put my finger on it.

As soon as I stop tugging, the image straightens out. It looks like a woman... Yes, it is a woman. I can't tell if she's Kurah or Poruah class. She's not fat, but she's not all bones either. Her hair is long and blonde, her eyes a vivid green. Her dress matches her eyes and waves like there is wind, but I feel none. A large emerald necklace sits just below her collarbone.

She smiles, and the feel of it makes me want to cry. To put my head on her shoulder and tell her my problems.

But I don't.

I back away.

People like this can't be trusted.

"Aren't we a shy one?" she says, her voice a smooth alto.

"Who are you?" I demand.

"You already sound like a queen."

I lift my chin, though all I want is to get away from this woman who seems to see into my soul.

"My... You're much different from your predecessors."

"You know about the other queens?" What am I saying? This is only a dream.

"I know about them all."

Sure she does. She knows as much as I do because she's a figment of my brain made excruciatingly real.

"I'm sorry about the nightmares," she says.

My imagination is sorry. How cute. It's much better than the nightmares themselves, though.

"You don't have to pretend to be strong around me."

"Who said anything about pretending?" I counter.

"You didn't have to say anything at all." She reaches toward me, but I jerk away.

"Don't touch me," I say.

"If it's a dream, why do you care?"

I feel for my daggers, but they aren't here. None of my weapons are. They're the one thing I can always count on in my dreams, and now they're gone.

"It doesn't matter," she says. "There's not much time left. I need you to know something."

I eye her, not trusting a thing that comes out of her mouth, even if she's my imagination. No one is to be trusted. "What?"

"I care about you. I'm sorry you wished to die, but I'm glad you didn't. I need you here. Please, fall asleep so you can come back to visit me tomorrow night." Her words roll off me.

"I don't know what you're talking about."

She ignores me. "It's good that you protected yourself when you were attacked. Keep that instinct. Keep it."

She fades back into fuzz. This time, I push the image away.

CHAPTER 10

FIRST THING THE NEXT MORNING, I'm fitted for new clothes. I stand in nothing but my underthings in the bedroom.

"Tut-tut," the seamstress says as she measures me. "Too skinny."

But it's muscle. I'm fast. I'm strong.

I'm not like anyone else here. I won't belong.

When the seamstress is done, half a dozen of my maids help me get ready for the day. I want to go back to bed. The process of getting ready is exhausting and too extensive. Of course, after my weird dream, I'm not sure how I feel about it. It's better than the terrors of blood and pain that rule my nightmares.

Clothing item after clothing item is buttoned and tied and corseted on—more than I've ever worn before at one time. Layers of jewels, hair, and makeup are added. It's too much. Nothing at all like who I am, but I let them for now. I'm tired of arguing, and they've been fairly strict about this. It's funny how pushy these women can be. It reminds me of Daros, but I don't want to think on him as they finish getting me ready.

I move to my sitting room, where Jem and another lady in waiting are sitting. They stand as I enter.

"Your Majesty." Jem curtsies. "We are here to teach you proper etiquette."

Joy. "Who is this with you?"

"Inyi, Your Highness," Jem replies.

There's a beauty to Inyi. Glowing skin. Golden brown hair and eyes. She looks as if the sun kissed her at birth.

"If you will follow us," Jem says.

They lead me out the door, and several bodyguards follow. I hate having them behind me, even if I can handle them. They could attack at any moment.

We wind through corridors that I know from the maps. When we come to a small room with a few chairs and a low table, we stop.

One of the guards goes in first, checking to make certain there's no one hiding. Once he gives the all clear and takes up residence outside the doorway, I trudge in. Though it's small, like I first thought, it's still bigger than my old bedroom. The typical landscape pictures hang on the cream-colored walls. The chairs are a dark-brown wood, wide but hard.

I remain standing, not wanting to sit in a hard chair, and they do the same. It's not that I can't handle a hard chair, it's that after everything I've been through, if I can avoid one, I will. "What about proper etiquette?" I ask.

"First off, you should sit, in consideration of us. We can't take a chair until you do," Jem says.

Not happening. These things are too uncomfortable. But if comfort is not a concern for them, who am I to stop them? "Sit."

"Your Majesty," Inyi says, "we couldn't possibly do so without you first taking a seat."

"Sit." My order rings out.

The girls settle down in two chairs against the wall, away from the window. Jem's lips thin. She's miffed. Too bad for her. Inyi is wide eyed, like she's stunned by my words.

"What else?"

"Your Majesty, a queen shows concern for those around her," Jem says. "She thinks of others."

"Why should I think of others, when they've never thought of me?" It's rude but true.

"Because you are their leader now," Inyi says. "Your thoughts should always be about them first."

Her words stir me. Not that I'd admit it. The queen has always been self-centered, even if she shows some outward caring like sitting for others to rest. "Moving on."

Jem opens her mouth like she's going to say more on the matter, but Inyi stops her with an elbow to the side. Jem glares at her but covers the expression.

"You must learn how to enter a room," Jem says. "When entering a room, the queen must first look to the right and then the left."

I snort. "Why?"

"Because"—she huffs—"*Your Majesty*, the higher the ranking official, the more to the right side of the room they are. They get closer to you the higher up they go. It's an honor and a privilege to have the right side directly next to the queen."

Layers of meaning that matter little to me. Those who are thought to be the highest ranking might be the biggest scum. "Give me something else."

Jem pulls her chin upward, making it wrinkle her chin. I'm getting to her. "You mustn't touch the back of a chair, even when sitting in it," she says.

This has to be a joke. The chairs are already torture devices, there's no sense in making them worse. "Why?"

She sputters.

Inyi says, "It isn't done. You need to appear regal and strong, no matter the circumstance. Sitting up tall and not relying on anything, even the back of a chair, proves this."

"It proves little." Except that one can sit in horrid situations for a long time. What's the point of that?

Inyi clears her throat. "Yes, well… Why don't you give it a try?"

"Are these the things you were learning to do before taking the Mortum Tura?"

"These are the basics," Jem says. "We learned so much more

over the years. Take me, for example. I've been studying to be queen since I was eight."

And I've been training to kill longer than that. "And you're how old now?"

"Twenty. Though I must say, Your Majesty, it's considered impolite to ask."

Ignoring her chiding, I say, "Why were you training when there was still a queen on the throne? Isn't that disloyal to the current queen?"

"Not at all. There are those training to be queen even now. We, ladies in waiting happened to be the ones who were ready to drink the Mortum Tura."

I focus my attention on her. "That doesn't explain how you remained loyal."

"We all know queens die quickly, Your Highness." She averts her gaze.

"Are you implying that I'm going to die soon?"

"Not at all"—her glare says otherwise; she'd see me dead now if she could—"But we should focus back on getting you up to par."

I let it drop. After all, I won't be around once I figure out who sent the assassin. Will I?

"Now, we must get you a pet," she says.

"What in all of Valcora would I do with a pet?"

"It shows your status. Only the wealthy have pets, because they can afford to. It would be most—"

"I know that," I say. "It doesn't answer why *I* should have one."

"You have enough wealth to display one now," Inyi says. "We could get you a tiger, a dog, a monkey, or any other animal you desire."

Another rule I won't follow. Daros said pets make you soft. Unable to do your job. I turn to face the window, eyes burning at the memory of how he made me kill a stray cat I brought home when I was little.

Nothing like that will ever happen again. "Moving on," I say.

"We need to think about your portrait," Jem says. "Queens have one made the first month of their reign."

I'm beginning to think there isn't a rule I will follow. "My likeness is not to be displayed in any way." Daros could find me and take me back.

"But Your Majesty," Inyi says, "the people need to see what you look like."

"I said *no*." My voice is sharper than I intended, but I can't risk him discovering where I am. No one can know I belonged to him. No one can know I am an assassin. It doesn't matter if the Mortum Tura chose me, the people will demand my death if they know I'm a killer instead of a ruler. My position is risky enough as it is.

Inyi starts to protest, but Jem stops her. "Let the queen think what she wants. We can only do our best to teach her our ways. If she won't have them, she won't last much longer."

I snort again. Like she knows how good my skills are.

"What next, Inyi?" Jem asks.

"You can't have anyone touch you, except servants helping you prepare yourself," the girl replies.

Maybe there's one rule I can follow. Unless they're trying to kill me. Then I can't promise anything.

"Which goes along with you not being able to marry," Jem says with glee.

I hadn't wondered why queens of Valcora don't take a husband. It never crossed my mind that it might be an actual rule. This one will be easy to acquiesce to.

"The queen can't have relations either." Jem grins.

"Why not?" Not that I was planning on having any.

"Because she's not allowed to have kids. The law doesn't want them to think they have a claim to the throne, when queens are made only through the Mortum Tura."

Something else I never thought of. But I don't want to think anymore. Not with Jem being snotty at every comment and with Daros at the top of my thoughts. It's a struggle to keep a placid face.

"We're done for the day," I say moving toward the door.

"But Your Majesty..." Inyi says.

"Let her go," Jem says. "If she doesn't want to learn our ways, she can fail without us."

Determined to ignore her, I take another step. A strange sensation flickers at my back, and I swing around just in time to see a man crashing through the window.

Jem and Inyi scream. I pull out two daggers, though not my poisoned one.

He runs toward me and jumps over the low table. I flash my blades before he reaches me. He has a sword in hand. I won't last long against that, but he can't take me; I want to know who sent him.

"Guards," Jem calls out.

The attacker thrusts his sword at me. I block it using my dagger, with little room to spare. With my other hand, I throw the second dagger. It lands in his shoulder.

I slowly circle him, intent on getting between him and my ladies in waiting. They may not be my favorite people, but there's no way their deaths will be on my hands. There's enough blood on my hands as it is.

My opponent grabs hold of the hilt of the dagger stuck in him and yanks it out of his shoulder with a grunt. Now he has two weapons. I pull out the dagger that was strapped to my thigh, to even the odds.

The man gives me a cruel smile and jumps forward, brandishing his weapons. Behind me, Inyi screams again.

"*Guards*," Jem yells.

My attacker shoves a chair toward the door, locking it under the handle. While he's distracted, I go at him and nick his waist. He roars, swinging his sword. I leap back and collide with one of the ladies in waiting. Someone props me back up. It's Jem. Inyi has fainted.

I'm surprised Jem hasn't as well, but there's no time to think about it. The man charges at me again. There's not much room to maneuver, with two chairs with girls in them at my back. I doubt he's going after them, but I can't give him leverage.

I throw another dagger at him. He blocks it with his sword, and it clatters to the ground.

There's a banging at the door. The chair in front of it vibrates but doesn't budge. I'm on my own, which would be easier if the weapons were even. I've faced worse odds, though.

The only dagger within easy reach is my poisoned one. I can't use it if I'm to question him. Just one blade it is. I dart forward and back, slicing his stomach before he can fully swing. He holds out his sword, but it's his other hand I'm worried about. He brings it back and pivots it forward, releasing my dagger back toward me.

I duck, heart pounding. Jem is still sitting, so the blade goes into the wall behind her, under a painting.

I spring to my feet, diving up and forward as I do so. My dagger barely misses my opponent's stomach. He thrusts his sword at me, and I bend back. Wind rustles across my chest, as the blade passes over it.

We spar, neither of us gaining an edge on the other. He's good. Too good. Did Daros train him? The thought makes me falter, and I almost get a cut to the arm. I flash my dagger up and stop the metal. My hand is twisted to the side, but I have the perfect opportunity to go for his face. I snake my arm forward.

Before I can get there, he brings his sword to my neck. The blade presses against my skin.

I lost.

I haven't been beaten outside of training. "Who sent you?" I ask.

The man laughs. Stupid man, laughing when he should be slitting my throat. I stab him in the arm holding the sword. He drops his blade with a howl, and I kick it across the room.

The chair in front of the door shudders. My attacker slinks away from me to dive for the sword. I have to get it before he does.

He bends down. I knee him in the face, but it's too late. Even as he falls backward, he has the sword in hand.

The door slams against the chair, opening a good inch. Inyi squeals, awake again. I rush toward my attacker, but his sword comes up, halting my progress. I'm tempted to throw my dagger, but then I'd only have the poisoned one in my boot.

My hands grow slick with sweat. I keep a good grip on my dagger—not too tight, not too loose.

He comes at me, swinging his sword like a madman and sending me scurrying backward. The length of his blade is going to do me in.

Though maybe not. His arm is dripping blood.

I get ready to throw my dagger, hoping to distract him long enough to wrestle the sword away from him.

The door bursts open. Three guards rush in, one after the other. My attacker glances toward them. I swing my arm back, and my opponent looks at me. The first guard doesn't hesitate, but stabs him right through the heart.

My attacker falls to the floor. Adrenaline pumps through me.

"We should have learned how to defend ourselves, instead of all these rules." Inyi's voice is slurred.

"Quiet," Jem says.

I'm surprised Jem isn't more squeamish. But then, she has lived at the palace for a while now. Perhaps she's used to this kind of thing.

"Forgive us for not being in here before he attacked you," the guard who stabbed the man says.

"Is he dead?" I ask.

The guard feels for a pulse, though it's obvious the man expired. "He is."

"Drat." It can't be helped now. I go about picking up my daggers and cleaning them. "What's your name?"

"Wilric, Your Highness. If I may, why do you have so many weapons?"

I remember Nash mentioning him. His bushy eyebrows are over dark eyes. Staring into them, I'm not sure he can be trusted, even if Nash said he could be. But Wilric did save my life. Unless he killed the attacker on purpose, so I couldn't interrogate him.

"Next time, injure my attackers," I say, ignoring his question. "Don't kill them."

He bows his head. "Yes, Your Majesty."

I glance down at the lifeless man. It's a shame I can't question him. I need to know who sent him. Is it the same person as last time? Someone new? Daros?

He can't have found me. He just can't.

I turn away. I don't know how, but the attacker knew how to find me. Someone has inside knowledge of my life.

And they will have to pay.

CHAPTER 11

Ranen stands as I enter my sitting room. "If you listened to me, you would be assaulted less," he says.

He just put himself up as being behind the threats on my life. But it could be Daros or someone else. I wish I had answers. "I want the furniture in this room changed to something comfortable as soon as possible."

"But, My Lady—"

"I am the queen. There is no *but*. Get a move on my request."

He clenches his teeth and leaves the room at a much slower pace than I would like. He's definitely one I'm going to have to watch out for.

I open the door to find a guard on each side of it, a woman and a man, but not the one from last night. Where is he?

Trying not to show signs of weakness, I tell the guards, "I wish to see my Head Advisor."

"Yes, My Lady." One of them bows and hurries off. Stupid, really. They should have a runner to do that, not the man who's supposed to be guarding my life. Either they have no clue, or they don't care about my life.

I'm not sure which one I prefer.

I wait in my sitting room, though I refuse to sit in one of those awful chairs. Several minutes later, someone knocks on the door. Finally.

"Come in," I call out.

Ranen opens the door, no furniture in sight.

"What are you doing back without my chairs?"

"You called for me."

"No. I sent you to fix my furniture problem."

"And then you sent for the Head Advisor. That's me."

Oh bother. "Not anymore. I demote you to Furniture Fixer." Even if he hates me for it, this is where he belongs. Even if it's not a position, I just made it one.

He pales. "But—"

"I told you, I am your queen. There are no *buts.*"

He puckers his lips like he ate something sour. "Yes, Your Highness." He bows and leaves the room. Again.

I want to stomp my foot. Instead, I poke my head back out my door. "What is your name?" I ask the guard who didn't fetch Ranen.

"Afet, Your Majesty."

"Afet, where is the guard who spoke with me last night? Nash?"

"I don't know, My Lady," the guard who went to find Ranen says.

"And your name?" I ask.

"Stird, Your Highness."

All this *My Lady* and *Your Highness* is getting as old as the bowing. "Well, go find him."

"Yes, My Lady," he says with a bow.

I slam the door. Hopefully that gets them moving. I don't understand anyone here. They're constantly bowing to me and calling me *Your Highness,* and yet no one seems to listen to me. I know nothing about being a queen—maybe that's the way it's supposed to work?

Maybe a queen has no real power and is more of a figurehead. With the way I've been treated so far, that's the only thing that makes sense. But then, why even have a queen? Why not a

60

governing council? Perhaps there is a simple reason, but I was never allowed to know much about politics.

The wait is worrisome. What if they can't find Nash? What if I don't see him again? He is the one person in this place who seems genuine so far. Not someone who might be threatening my life. Plus, he's not annoying.

I pace my room, thinking over the attack as I wait. Was it Daros who sent the assassins? For all I know, it could be someone else entirely. Without knowing who's behind them, I can't stop the next one. Perhaps I couldn't stop it even if I knew, but there would be some comfort in it. I need to figure it out so I can get on with my life. Or my possible death.

There's a knock on the door.

"Come in," I call, hoping Ranen doesn't pop his head in this time. Unless he has good furniture, that is.

Nash opens the door.

"Good. Shut the door behind you," I say.

He does so and says, "I heard you were attacked again. Are you all right?"

"Fine. Why didn't you come this morning, like I asked?"

"I'm glad you're well. Wilric did a good job saving you. He should be rewarded."

Maybe he should be. Then again, maybe he was protecting himself. "You didn't answer my question."

"I didn't come because no one believed you asked me to."

"But I made you Head Advisor."

"No one believed that either."

"Well, why not?"

"Because no one heard you say it. If you want people to believe it, then you need to decree it in public."

"Arrange to have everyone there, and I'll make it official."

"That's the problem—I can't arrange it now. No one will listen to me."

I growl in frustration and head for the door. There are too many skirts on me. The two guards still stand outside my door. "I want

an audience with the most important people in this government," I
say. "Can you do that?"

They look at each other. The one on my right says, "I
don't know."

"Find someone that can and make it happen." I slam the door.

Hopefully my furniture comes before the people do. I don't
want to have a meeting in my bedroom, but I swear I won't sit in
one of those chairs. It's like they purposefully gave me a room I'd
be uncomfortable in.

"May I make a suggestion?" Nash asks.

"Only if you tell me your last name first."

"Will you tell me your name?"

"I did tell you I don't have one."

"You were being serious?" His brows lift.

"I was."

"What have people in your life called you?" He looks
perplexed.

If I wasn't so accustomed to it, I'd find it perplexing too. "Nothing, really. Sometimes *girl*. Nothing of any significance that I'd
want to continue to be called."

"We should find you a name before the meeting."

"Is that what your suggestion was?"

"No."

"Then tell me your last name, and you can make your
suggestion."

"Zorris. It's Nash Zorris. And I most kindly advise that you use
this meeting to understand the other members of government."

"I don't care about them." I don't care about any of this. Mostly
I want everyone to leave me alone.

"I know. You can even let them know that, but I strongly
recommend you start getting to know them. Some will be allies,
but others will want you off the throne and they'll do anything
they can to make it so."

"They can have the throne. I don't want it." I'm surprised I
admitted that out loud, but it's more than true. If I'm going to trust
someone, it may as well be this Nash.

"The only way they can get you off the throne is if you're dead," he says.

I want to say that it doesn't matter. Death would be welcome. That's why I got into this mess in the first place. Yet... someone tried to take my life, and I wouldn't let them. That has to mean that I care. Right?

And there was something about that dream last night. Something that scared me, but at the same time I thought I should embrace. Something kind and loving. Something unlike anything I've ever felt before.

I pace the room. Nash is thankfully silent.

I don't know what to do.

The pacing doesn't help. It only makes me feel more restless. What I want is to spar with someone. To fight. There's no room for that in here without moving furniture, though I do wonder if Nash would brawl with me. This is off topic and not very useful when I need to decide if I want to live or not.

My life... it's not worth living. Not after what I've done—the blood I've spilled.

Yet I can't bring myself to say I want to die. It shocks me. How did I come to this point?

It doesn't matter. It's what I need, and now that I want to live, I will cling to life.

"What if I don't want them to kill me?" I ask.

Nash crinkles his eyebrows together. "I'll protect you, and so will others. But this is exactly why you need to try to get to know the leaders in government. They can make or break you."

There's a knock on the door. I open my mouth to call out, but Nash puts up a hand to stop me. "Please. Allow me to answer it."

I nod, conceding to him in this. He does seem to know a lot more about how a queen should act than I do. It's not what I was trained in. What was he trained in, to know all this as a guard?

He opens the door and speaks to someone I can't see. Once he closes the door again, he turns to me and says, "The council is ready for you."

And I am most certainly not ready for them.

CHAPTER 12

IT'S NOT AN OVERLY large room, but big enough to make me wary of all the people in it. About twenty men and women. I'm the youngest of the group.

They bow as I enter. After I motion for them to rise, I want to ask Nash if this is truly the entire government. My training flares to life and I imitate them, holding my shoulders back and head high. Each of them seems like they have abundant ego to fill this palace. They remind me of my old master.

But I don't want to think of him.

Him forcing me in a tiny closet with glass jutting out on all sides, for hours at a time.

Him forcing me to stab rats.

Him tying me up until I freed myself, however long it took.

I shake my head. I'd rather force myself to get familiarized with all of these men and women than think of him again. And that's what I'm going to do.

I make my way to the chair Nash guides me to. Ranen sits on my right. *Suck up.* He should be out, finding my new chairs, instead of here. At least this chair doesn't look quite so torturous.

As soon as I'm seated, everyone else takes a seat.

Then they all look at me.

What are they doing that for? *Oh.* I'm probably expected to lead this meeting? I motion to Nash. "This is the new Head Advisor, Nash. You will all treat him as such. If not, it will be off with your head."

There are several gasps throughout the room, but I don't catch who they come from. Ranen clutches at the arms on his chair, knuckles turning white.

I should make sure he's put in his place. I motion to him. "This is my new furniture arranger. He will be going throughout the palace, making certain the furniture is comfortable."

There are a few more gasps but also a few titters. I refrain from smiling.

Nash cuts in after that, and I'm grateful for his help. I don't know how to talk to these people, but he seems to. "The queen would like you each to state your name and tell her a bit about your position."

The man next to Ranen starts. "Your Majesty, I am your most humble of servants." Yeah. Seems like it. The guy has a triple chin and sounds as if he thinks he's king of another country, voice pompous and commanding. "I am Timit of the most noble house of Alek. I am Head of the Treasury and at your service for whatever you may need."

I'm sure he does a great job of lining his pockets, if he's the one responsible for all the taxes on all classes. Were those the last queen's idea, or some combination of the two? As a nation, we have lots of rich mines, but as a people, most are poor. Where is it all going? I'll have to find out. Before I can think any more on it, the next person is introducing herself.

"I am Yuka, Your Highness. I am Head of the Arts." Her sleek black hair is pulled into an elaborate bun, letting her green eyes stand out.

Is she the reason there are portraits of landscapes everywhere?

"I'm Borkus, Your Highness, of the house of Prenton. Head of Design." He has a wide forehead and bulging lips.

"And what do you do?" I ask.

"I am over the court's clothing. I set trends and styles."

65

There's someone I should fire. Too much poof and layers. A thin pair of slacks suits me fine. I focus on the next person. The thinnest man here, though filled with muscles.

"I am Jaku, Head of the Guard, Your Majesty." His voice is deep.

"You're the one who has to answer for the attacks on my life," I say.

He hesitates. "Eh…yes. I suppose I am."

I purse my lips and tap them with a finger. I could rail at him for letting the assassins through, but perhaps it's best not to do that in front of others. When I turn my attention away from him, I see him out of the corner of my eye, letting out a great exhale.

"I am Kada, Head of Relations with the Queen, Your Majesty." Though she's sitting, she appears short, with her blonde hair barely reaching Jaku's shoulder.

Another lackluster performance. There's been almost no communication between the palace government and me up until this point. And *I* called this meeting. What is it with these people? "Why have you not called a meeting sooner?"

Her gaze darts to Ranen and back to me. "I… uh… thought you didn't want a meeting."

I didn't, but that's not her or Ranen's decision to make. "In the future, you will communicate directly with me or Nash," I say.

Kada gives an eager nod. "Yes, Your Majesty."

I focus on the next councilwoman.

"I am Monkia. Head of Staff, Your Highness," the older woman with gray hairs blending with her dark hair says.

"And I am Nidon, Your Majesty. Head of Food and Commerce." His weight rivals that of the triple-chin man.

Another person who needs to be replaced with someone who can better accomplish the job. Though the famine is over, food isn't properly distributed. I didn't have enough on the streets, though that might be my own doing since I was avoiding taking care of myself properly.

"Your Majesty, I am Sidle. Head of Military." He reminds me of Daros—thick, yet there's the impression of hidden muscles.

I'll be avoiding him.

In the middle of the group at the other side of the room is a peaked woman with a fringe of red hair. "I'm Mina, Your Highness. Head of Foreign Relations."

The assistants come next, starting with Mina's gawky male aide. The next person goes, and the next. All helpers in one way or another.

I've been bored for some time. It's boring to listen to so many people talk and keep track of who belongs with what name and occupation. I always had a hard time concentrating when lecture time came. Hopefully Nash can give me a few pointers later that make more sense.

A while later, the last person finishes. He is on the left, a ways from me.

Nash looks at me like he expects something. They all do. Only problem is I have no idea what.

"And your name, Your Majesty?" Yuka asks.

A memory hits me so hard, I feel like I've been slapped—Daros telling me I'm worth nothing. Not even a name.

"That's all for now," I say, hoping it dissuades them from asking again. I could continue the meeting, but I've gotten more than I came for. "You're dismissed."

I stand, and they bow again. I leave, and Nash follows me out. Despite the steps forward I'm taking, I feel as lost and hopeless as ever.

CHAPTER 13

THAT NIGHT, as I ready for bed, I notice the sleeping gown the servants brought for me fits. I dismiss them and search my drawers. They're full to brimming. Someone—or several someones—must have worked overtime to get this accomplished.

There are frills and fluff and too much volume. One dress could easily turn into five. Whoever picked out this wardrobe has no idea what I like.

I sit on the bed. It's too soft. The floor would be better. Still, I don't move.

Maybe if I lie down, I won't be able to fall asleep.

No nightmares, then.

I could go out and about again, but I'm too exhausted. What a day it's been...

I give in and curl up on my side. I haven't felt anything like it before. It's like being scooped up by a cloud. Last night, I slept the night sitting up against the headboard, too distraught to pay attention to the bed, but now it's all I can think about.

I toss and turn, grateful sleep isn't coming yet. If I hold off till I'm exhausted, I may be able to get some rest without horrid dreams.

Not likely, but one can hope.

I kick the covers off, and a cool breeze inches across my skin.

The world is fuzzy again, like someone punched me in the head too hard. Only my head doesn't hurt. The haze goes away more quickly than last time, revealing the same lady in green.

"Who are you?" I ask.

"Who are you?" she responds.

"I don't know."

"Then I'm not ready to tell you either."

"Why do you keep coming to my dreams?" *Though this is only the second one, it seems to be a thing with her.*

"I'm better than nightmares. Am I not?"

With a sigh, I sit, hovering on something I can't see. I take a look around for the first time. There's nothing here but the colors of a sunset, blurred together like a cloud. It's a dream world, for certain.

"What do you know of my nightmares?" I ask.

"I know they're violent and leave you awake more than they should," she says. "And I know keeping you from sleep keeps us from talking. I need you to sleep more. We'll progress faster if you do."

I don't want to sleep. Besides, I was trained to only sleep a handful of hours. "Progress at what?"

"Are you going to start sleeping more?"

The nightmares come to mind, and I shudder. "I can't."

"Then that's what we'll work on first—getting you to sleep more."

"Why do my dreams suddenly want me to sleep more?" I ask, trying to figure out what my subconscious is telling me.

"It's no trick."

I almost ask her how she knows what I'm thinking, but then I remember this isn't real. Of course my own mind knows what I'm thinking.

"If you're not stronger, I won't be able to hold the nightmares off. That will cause problems for the two of us."

"You're holding off my nightmares?" *I want it to be true, but how can my imagination do such a thing?*

"With a little bit of magic."

I gasp. "Magic? I thought it was extinct."

Why would my subconscious conjure that up?

"It isn't gone. It's almost everywhere now, from what I gather. There's a little that controls this country, though. If you think long enough, you'll know what it is."

Why are my thoughts taking me here? I haven't thought of magic before.

"Maybe you should. After all, it governs your life now."

"You mean the chalice? The Mortum Tura?"

"Very good. You're a quick learner," she says. "The Mortum Tura has magic. Its influence will grow every time you drink it."

How do I know all this? I could be making it up.

"But you're beginning to believe I'm something other than you, aren't you?"

I don't need to answer that for her to know what's going on.

"I knew you were a quick study."

"Do I want to drink the Mortum Tura as often as I can?"

"Yes, but be careful. It's a lot to take in at once." She grows fuzzy.

"Wait. We were just getting into our conversation."

Her voice grows fainter. "Which is why you need to get more sleep."

She fades out altogether, joining the colors of the sunset.

CHAPTER 14

AFTER LAST NIGHT, I could use some good news. Everything seems foggier this morning, but I still remember the strange dream. And the one before. It's the second time in a long while that I haven't had a nightmare. No blood. No screams. No tainted daggers. Just blissful silence.

I should be grateful, but instead I'm worried. What is holding them back? And what if whatever it is stops and they return fiercer than ever?

There's a knock on the door, and I wish Nash was here to answer it for me. My servants are gone. My fault for ordering them away, but they were bothering me with their constant pecking at me. There's no one to hide behind. Not that I ever needed to hide behind anyone.

"Enter."

Nash strides in and closes the door behind him. I haven't seen him since I left the meeting yesterday. More like ran from it. He must have sensed my mood, because he left me at my rooms without a word.

He sits in the chair he used before. "You did very well yesterday."

"Well? I can't remember a thing from it."

"We'll work on it. The important thing is you asserted your authority in front of all of them."

"How old are you?"

"I'm nineteen."

"You talk like a forty-year-old."

"Only to you."

"And why is that?" I demand.

"Because you chose me to be your advisor. I'm doing the best I can."

I want to compliment him on a job well done, but I hold back the awkward words. "How are we going to work on me not remembering who is who?"

"One person at a time."

"You're very helpful," I say.

There's another knock on the door, and Nash answers it. "It's your ladies in waiting," he says to me.

"Tell them I'm busy." Hopefully that keeps them away.

He does so and returns to his position. "Let's start with those you do know."

"Ranen."

"Good. You know your furniture master. Who else?"

Was that sarcasm? His straight face makes it difficult to tell. I shrug, wishing I had a way to be more confident. I remember faces and degrees of mistrust I felt for them; that's about it.

"Let's figure it out. The first person introduced yesterday—do you remember what he looked like?"

"Yes. Three chins and wig-like hair."

He purses his lips, like he's trying to keep from laughing. "And his name is…?"

"T something. Tem?"

"Timit."

"All right, Timit, then." I'm grateful they didn't introduce themselves with their last names too. Gives me less to keep track of.

"Anyone else you remember?"

"Something like a Minx?"

Again, he struggles to control the twitching of his lips. "You mean Mina?"

"Yes, her."

"Good. What does Mina do?"

"Sit far away from me?" Though I'm not at all certain.

"She does that, but why? What's her position? Why does she matter to the state?"

"Because she's different looking than the rest?" With her pale skin and red hair, she has to be memorable in some way even if I can't remember her name.

"She's Head of Foreign Relations."

I growl. "There's no way I can remember this all. Even if I do, what's the point?"

"The point is you do your job."

"It's not a job I wanted."

He cocks his head to the side. "If you didn't, why did you drink the Mortum Tura?"

"It's not like you'd understand."

"Try me." His voice is dry.

"I'd rather not."

He sighs. "For wanting me as your advisor, you sure don't give me a lot of information."

"You're the one who's supposed to give me information," I say, hoping to deter him from wanting to know me better.

"But if you'd tell me more, I could give you better, more accurate information."

"I'm not telling you more, no matter how hard you try to get me to."

"It might feel good to open up to someone."

"I'm not doing it."

"I don't want to fight. Let's continue with the lesson. Who came after Timit?"

I'd rather keep fighting. It's so much more interesting than politics. But we continue on with the names and positions anyway. How it all correlates together and what I need to do about it. Time creeps by at a pace a snail could beat.

My answers become automatic, even if not always right, but I'm not focusing on what's going on. There are too many other things to worry about for me to care who is called what. Such as who's trying to kill me and how they're getting to me.

"And who is Jaku?" Nash asks.

"That I remember. Head of the Guard. Arrange a meeting with him for me."

He lifts an eyebrow but says, "As you wish."

There's yet another knock on the door, this one a swift, sure two-pound knock. Nash moves to answer it. I straighten my shoulders and hold my lips tight together.

Nash admits Ranen into the sitting room where I venture in, followed by several footmen carrying chairs and a sofa. I want to gush over how comfortable they look. Instead, I hold my position and let them take the old furniture away.

"Where would you like the new furniture, my lady?" Ranen asks, voice brisk.

"As it was before." Because I don't know what else to tell him.

A footman and Ranen spend the next several minutes rearranging the furniture. I have to hold myself back to keep from helping them. I'm not used to keeping from such tasks.

Then again, I'm not used to a lot of things.

When they're finished, Ranen bows at me. "I hope Your Ladyship approves of the new furniture. I have begun to have new ones installed around the palace."

"Very well. You can go," I say.

He narrows his eyes at me, deep-seated anger burning in his gaze. But still, he bows again and makes his way out of my sitting room.

"Finally." I plop down into the closest chair. "Much better."

Nash remains standing, giving me a look I have a hard time understanding.

"What is it?" I demand.

"He's trying to win back your good graces, and you ignored all he's done."

The usual feeling of shame burns through me at having done

something wrong, but I was taught long ago not to show it. "I don't care for the man."

"No one does, but he holds many favors from different people both in and out of government. You'd do well to treat him better. I fear you're making an enemy of him, and that could have dire consequences."

I shrug him off. "Let them try to kill me."

"They already are."

I clamp my mouth shut, looking for something to change the subject to. There's a glimmer as a ring on his finger catches the sunlight streaming in through the window. "Where did you get that ring? It doesn't seem like something a guard would have," I say.

He hesitates a moment. "It's not. It was given to me by my father."

"Do you mind if I look at it?"

He holds his hand out to me. It's a silver ring, chunky and masculine even while it holds a ruby in the center of it. It's not gaudy, but neither is it plain.

"Why would your father give you such an item if you have no cause to use it as a guard?" I ask.

His hesitation is longer this time. "Technically, he didn't give it to me. He died, and my mother insisted I have it, as his only son."

I don't know what to say to that. I study the ring, wondering what stories it possesses. What it knows about Nash. "I'm sorry you lost your father. Do you want to tell me about it?"

He drops his hand. "It was to almaca."

The disease that often kills those who contract it. "During the famine or more recently?"

"It was last year." His voice is so quiet; I strain to hear him.

Yet another knock interrupts the moment. As Nash goes to open it, I resume my pretentious royal posture, hoping it's not Ranen back again. I'm not ready to play nice with him. I doubt I ever will be.

Nash turns to me. "There's a visitor here to see you. He says he knows you, but he's not from the palace. He's got enough rank that he made it all the way up here and requested an audience."

I refrain from biting my lip. "I know no one." Except one person. One I never wanted to see again.

Nash lifts an eyebrow. "Should I send him away?"

I open my mouth to say *yes*, but what comes out is, "No. Let him in."

My knees shake as Nash moves aside so the person can come in.

It's as I feared.

My old master walks into the room.

CHAPTER 15

"NASH, OUT." My knees shake harder, but I keep my voice firm.

Though he looks like he'd rather stay, Nash gives a bow and is out the door.

"What are you doing here?" I demand of Daros.

My old master is in his prime, rounded but with hidden muscles. He has shrewd dark eyes under thick eyebrows. More worrisome are his hidden cunning and cruelty. "You didn't think I would stay away," he says.

"I left you, Daros. Washed my hands of anything to do with you."

"And yet, you came here. Took the Mortum Tura. Became queen."

I stand, pulling myself up to my full height. "I did what I had to do."

He smirks. "And look where it got you."

My knees shake so bad now, I'm afraid I'm going to fall back into my chair. At least my skirts are full enough to hide it. Never thought I'd be happy about such full skirts, though they're also useful for hiding weapons.

"What do you want?" My words come out more as a hiss than speech, but I can't help it.

"What do you think I want?" He smirks like he has me right where he wants me.

I have to fight against him. I did it once. Can I do it again? "There's nothing here for you."

He steps closer, his height towering over me. I want to shrink. To collapse. Instead, I force myself to remain steady and tall.

"Everything I want is here, at your finger tips," he says.

My breath is coming in short gasps. *At my fingertips.* He wants to control me. I can't handle this.

But I have to. If he gains command of me again, what will happen? To the country? An assassin queen? The Shadow Wraith as their ruler? No one will want me around—not that they do anyway, but it will be worse if I'm under his control. If I'm killing for him again.

"This is perfect. I groomed you to be a leader, and a leader you are," Daros says.

The last thing he groomed me to be is a leader. He may have taught me to emulate those around me. To blend in or stand out, depending on the needs. To fight for my life. But to lead? No. Not that. He was too busy stomping all over me whenever I did something wrong.

"You are right. I'm the queen. Get out and never come back," I say.

"Do you really think you can get rid of me so easily when I know all your secrets?"

I need to hold onto something, but the short table before me is of no use. I want to fall onto it and cry.

But there's no crying.

Not ever.

"You think you know my secrets," I counter. I wonder what would happen if I called to have him arrested. He'd probably kill me before I finished the sentence.

He scoots closer. "You've been hiding things from me?" He reaches for where I know he hides one of his many daggers.

I work to keep my breathing even. To not flinch or show a shred of the turmoil rumbling inside me.

"Never mind." He moves his hand away from his dagger. "I know enough. You will let me into your new life sooner or later. Now, about the law concerning taxes..."

He's going to try to control me again.

"What could you want to change about the laws?" The words spew from me. "Wait. I don't want to know. I don't want to have anything to do with you."

Before I know it, a blade is pressed against my gut.

"You will do what I tell you to." His voice is low. Menacing.

I can't help it. I laugh—a cold, unfeeling sound. "Or what? You'll kill me? Don't you think there's a reason I'm here?"

He takes his time sheathing his dagger. "There are worse things I could do than kill you."

Without meaning to, I shrink back. He gives a low chuckle and threads his fingers through my hair before yanking it back. He brings his face close to mine as I work not to clench my jaw. To not give way to the pain ratcheting through me.

"You are as weak as ever. You're nothing without me to command you, and you know it." He releases me with a jerk.

I stumble and knock into my chair before balancing myself. The threat of what he could do to me is enough to make me back down. To make me want to give into all of his demands.

But I promised not to kill again.

And now, I promise not to let him have control of my country. For it is mine.

I straighten to my full height, ignoring the roiling in my stomach. "You are not welcome here."

"Do not go trying to boss me around, girl. Just because you escaped from me once doesn't mean you have any hold over me. I'm the one with all the power, no matter what you may try."

"No. No more." My voice is halting.

"Don't you dare talk to me like that. You will listen to what I have to say and will follow through."

Putting all my might into it, I shove him away. He wavers, mouth hanging open.

"No," I say again. The word is stronger this time. Firm.

"You will not stand up to me." He takes a step forward, once again reaching for his dagger.

"*Nash*," I call out, hoping he can hear me. My heart drums within my chest.

The door bursts open. "Yes, my lady?"

"See to it that this… gentleman is shown off the property. Get some guards to do it." I tuck my hands into the folds of my skirt so their trembling can't be seen.

"Of course, Your Majesty."

"You'll regret this," Daros says, voice low enough only I can hear.

"I think not," I say.

Nash grabs my old master by the upper arm and yanks him out the door. I hear Nash out in the hall say, "Take him out to the streets and see that he doesn't return anytime soon."

I'm grateful for Nash taking it further than my fear let me go, though I doubt it will stop Daros from getting what he wants out of me. He always does, whatever his goal is—something to do with the new law concerning taxes, getting his Shadow Wraith back, and control. Who wouldn't want control over a kingdom?

Besides me. Except, I might not want it, but I think I'll be all be right with it.

I'm even more grateful that Nash passed the duty onto another guard. He comes back in the room, shuts the door, and hurries over to me. I fall back into the chair, and Nash kneels beside me. I feel sick, like I'm going to lose the contents of my stomach any second now.

"Did he hurt you?"

I laugh—a cold sound. "As much as he could in the few minutes he had."

Nash begins looking me over for injuries. "Where is it? I'll have his head."

"He didn't physically injure me," I say, though that doesn't stop him from touching me. It feels nice. I didn't know another person's touch could feel so…

Tender.

Soft.

Awakening.

It's unfathomable, and yet, I feel it. I don't understand.

Finally he seems satisfied that I really am not injured, and he lets go of me with a jolt. "Sorry. I shouldn't touch you. Please forgive me."

I shrug. Not like I'm about to tell anyone, after what that felt like. "It's forgotten and will stay that way for everyone." It's not like I'm about to have the first person I almost trust killed off just because our skin came in contact.

"Thank you." He meets my gaze, searching for something. "Who was that?"

"No one of importance."

"By the way you were trembling you can't tell me that."

I pull my shoulders back. "No one of importance. We'll leave it at that." If only I could keep him that way. Daros was like a father to me. A cruel father, but one nevertheless.

My everything.

My world.

I let him teach me things no one should learn. Make me do things no one should do. And now I hate myself for it.

Though not as much as I hate him.

CHAPTER 16

NASH IS POLITE, but distant. I wonder what he's thinking, but it's hard to focus on that. My jitters from seeing Daros are too great. I shouldn't have let him enter. It doesn't matter, though. Even if I didn't let him in, he'd find a way to me, and it would end much worse.

Not that I left him on a good note. He's bound to be raging now. I clench my fists just thinking about it. I've dealt with his wrath too many times for it not to affect me.

There's a knock at the door of my sitting room. I clamp my jaw shut. They wouldn't let Daros back in, would they? He can't have gotten his claws in the guards this fast. Unless they were there to begin with.

I stand, unwilling to face him sitting down. I force my fists to relax, taking three even breaths to calm myself.

"That should be Jaku, Head of the Guard," Nash says, speaking for the first time in several minutes. "He's here for the meeting you requested. Would you like me to leave you to it?"

I'm so thankful it's not Daros. I sink into my seat. There's a note of something in Nash's voice. A distance. I wonder if I hurt his feelings, sending him away when I was agitated before. "Please remain."

His lips twitch, but that's the only hint I get to what he's thinking. He bows deep from the waist and goes to open the door. "Presenting Jaku Hanka, Your Majesty."

Jaku walks in, his presence commanding, if not as great as Daros's. He has dark-brown eyes, brown hair, and a smile that doesn't look as if it belongs to the Head of the Guard. It's too sweet. Nash shuts the door behind him.

Jaku bows. After I tell him to stand, he says, "Your Majesty wishes to speak with me."

"I did. Sit." He chooses the chair directly across from mine, though it's the whole length of the room away, and I continue. "I want to know why the assassins were able to attack me."

He pales but doesn't shrink. "I'm afraid Your Majesty can lay the blame on me. Our guards noticed nothing out of the ordinary. All I can think is that the first used a secret path that is unknown to me. The second one broke through our lines, knocking out the guards so they couldn't come after him."

"Are his words true, Nash?"

If Nash is surprised by my inviting him into the conversation, he doesn't show it. "He speaks the truth, My Lady. I was on guard that day and saw nothing out of the ordinary. I questioned those around me, but no one else saw anything either."

He went so far as to question his peers. Interesting. Perhaps I was wiser than I thought, picking him as Head Advisor. Not that I put much thought into it, other than the feeling that I could trust him. It's probably wrong; that feeling always is. Still, I don't regret it.

"How can we find these secret tunnels, to keep this from happening again?" I put my life on the line enough as it is. I don't want someone else taking it from me. At least, that's what my actions say.

"There's no guarantee we will find something new, Your Majesty," Jaku says. "Forgive me for being so forward, but people have been trying for generations to find all the secret passageways in and out of this place, and they have yet to succeed."

"I prefer forward people. I feel we must try to find those

passages, though. In places I will frequent, if not elsewhere as well."

A muscle in Jaku's cheek twitches, but he appears calm otherwise. "I promise to do what I can, Your Majesty."

Is that enough? "What do you think, Nash?"

"I agree with Jaku. We can do our best."

"The first time I was attacked was in the queen's bathing area, and no one saw anything suspicious. Either someone is lying or there is at least one secret tunnel in there." Not that I will ever go back there. As relaxing as the bath was, I don't trust the place.

"I will send my best men to comb the area," Jaku says. "Except for Nash, as I recently had to relinquish him to you." He sounds rather put out.

"Nash has been a great asset." Though he bombards me with boring information, he's the only person in this place who seems to care enough to give me that information. Whether or not I'm interested in it or ready to use it is a different question entirely.

"I'm certain he has been, Your Highness," Jaku says.

I study the Head of the Guard. Is he hiding something? Silly question—everyone is hiding something. But is he hiding something that could affect my life? No way to tell. He holds my gaze steady and surely doesn't act like a common criminal. He probably has enough experience to obscure such things.

"If you're certain there's nothing else you'd like to add, Jaku, you're free to go," I say.

He stands and bows. "Please let me know if there's any further way I can assist you, Your Majesty."

Nash opens the door for him, then closes it after him. "Forgive me, my lady. I didn't know you were going to question him on the attack."

"What did you think I wanted?"

"Truthfully, I thought you were going to release him from his position."

"Why would I do that?"

"Most queens change the heads of their departments. The

guard is usually the first to go. Plus, the attacks happened on his watch."

The thought didn't cross my mind, other than with Ranen. He's the only one who makes my skin crawl to that point. Not that I trust the others, but there's no sense replacing someone I don't trust with another I don't trust either. Besides, I know no one to take the jobs. "Is that what you wanted to happen?"

"No, Your Majesty. I believe Jaku will serve you well enough."

Well enough. Now there's an endorsement if I ever heard one. I'll have to keep an eye on him. I'll have to keep an eye on them all if I want to be safe. The thought alone exhausts me. I'm used to obeying orders. This role is far beyond me.

"Is there anything you need?" He's closer than before, his voice soft.

I can only stare. Is he serious?

"Anything at all?" he asks.

Words finally come to me. "Why do you ask?"

"Because you are my queen. I promised to serve you, and…"

When he doesn't finish, I say, "And what?"

He shakes his head. "I will help you any way you need, Your Majesty."

It seems like there's more he's not saying. I wonder but don't feel like pushing. Not now, when there are assassins after me. I have to find out who's leading them, not spend time finding out more about Nash.

Killers after the Shadow Wraith, though I doubt they know it's so. I didn't think the day would ever come. Daros always protected me from others coming after me. Threatened them if anything happened to my life. They didn't know who I was, just that I was untouchable.

Such thoughts do me no good. I need to focus on the here and now. "Thank you for your willingness. The only thing I need is to find out who is sending these assassins."

"I will do everything in my power to help you find them."

Something about the tone of his voice has me believing him, whether that's smart or not.

CHAPTER 17

THE WORLD IS BARELY FUZZY this time. The woman in green comes into clarity and immediately asks, "Who are you?"

I sigh. "I'm no one."

"Then, for now, I'm no one as well," she says. "You didn't come to bed early."

"The city lights are much more interesting to watch."

"And yet, you still didn't have a nightmare."

It's true. Three nights in a row. How can that be?

"I told you—magic. It's time you start believing what I tell you. We're working up to that, aren't we?"

"Maybe." She doesn't feel like me. Or talk like me. And she knows things I don't.

"Exactly. It's time to trust that this is a real experience, even if you're sleeping," she says. "It can't take long for you to trust me on this; there's too much for us to do."

"Why can't we do it now?"

"Very well, then. Who is Daros? Even being here, I can't tell who he is. You keep it so closed up."

"My old master."

"I know that much, but your old master of what?"

I feel someone searching. Looking hard inside me. It's a peaceful, unobtrusive touch.

I wake.

That was not what I expected. Why did my dream end differently this time? Whatever the reason, I'm done with sleep for now. I don't care how nice the lady in green seems, there are some places I don't go.

I could tell her about the trainings. They weren't all bad. They weren't good either. My muscles are hardened with years of experience. But what good would it be to tell a dream figure that? Besides, I hate what I am.

I get down on the floor and start doing push ups, not caring about my night gown. I spend spare moments snatching what exercise I can. I have to keep my body in peak physical condition, though there isn't as much time to do it as before.

I blot my forehead. What's more than not wanting to tell the lady in green, I didn't like her searching my thoughts, even if she was gentle about it.

No one is allowed into my memories. Not even me.

At least, not without consequences.

CHAPTER 18

I'M SITTING in one of my new chairs, with Nash across from me. He's attempting to teach me more of what I need to learn, but I can't concentrate. My meeting with Daros is still in my mind. I need him out of there. The lady in green makes thoughts of him come even more frequently.

"We should work on conversations," he says.

I stare at him.

"Don't you think?" he asks.

"What about them?"

"How you converse with others is important. It can show a lot of grace and decorum or it can be crass and unappealing."

"Did someone put you up to this?" I can't imagine him coming up with it on his own.

"It doesn't matter. What's important is your words. Do you think what you just said would be acceptable among the Kurah class?"

"Who was it? Jem?"

"You didn't answer my question."

"Jem, then. Good to know."

"No," he says with a sigh. "It wasn't Jem. I answered your question. Will you answer mine?"

I tap a finger to my lips, pushing back thoughts of Daros. "One of the other ladies in waiting?"

"It was my mother. All right?"

Not what I was expecting. "Why did your mother suggest such a thing?"

"She's not a royal, but she used to be a servant for Queen Amily. She knows things."

"And she thinks I need better conversational skills?"

He shifts in his chair. "She suggested some topics that would help you learn your place better."

I don't like the sound of that. "I can speak on any topic well enough when I feel like it." I was trained to fit in. "I've been thinking."

"Yes?" Nash sounds exasperated.

It's time to change the subject to something I care about, to thoughts of my own instead of on Daros. There's one thing that might work. "I am the queen of Valcora. It's time I act like it."

"How so?"

It's something I have to think about. What difference can I make as royalty? "I want to get to know the people."

He relaxes back into his chair. "I think it's only fitting, since you've barely left your rooms since you became queen."

I try to ignore the rebuke.

"Didn't you know the people when you were out among them?" he asks.

I don't want to get into just how little I interacted with them. Just how little I was a part of anything that didn't have to do with killing. "I didn't know them as their queen."

"Hmm."

"I think it fitting I do so now."

"What did you have in mind?" he says after a moment's pause.

"A ball," I say.

"A ball?"

"Isn't that what royalty does?" I ask.

"Royalty, yes, but it doesn't seem very *you*."

"What would be more *me*?"

"I haven't figured that out yet."

Well, that's the most unhelpful thing I've heard all day. "Well, until you do, a ball it will be."

"A coronation ball, I should think," Nash says.

"I haven't heard of one of those. Why is that?"

"Not all queens live long enough to be coronated, but we'll make certain you do," he says, face serious.

He wants me to live.

The realization warms me to the core. *Someone wants me to live.* But now's not the time to grow mushy. "How much time do you think is needed for someone to plan?"

"I haven't a clue. But we'll say a week. Preferably two."

"Fine. Two weeks. Use all the help you need. I doubt you've planned a ball before."

"No, but I do have sisters obsessed with things like this. They bore me to tears talking about them."

That's new. "Would they be willing to help?"

"They'd be overjoyed. But they aren't part of your royal entourage, nor have they ever planned anything so big."

"I don't care about such trifles."

"Very well. I'll have them assist along with the servants. I'll see if I can find someone who's thrown a ball to help."

"You are close to your sisters?" I wonder what it would be like to have a family. I never had one, besides Daros. Not that he makes for a real family.

"Closer when I lived by them. They are in the city, and I live in the bunks with the guards," Nash said.

"Why are you still there?"

"I'm comfortable there."

"Well, if you ever want a room, commandeer whichever you want."

"Even this one?" he asks with a twinkle in his eye.

"Except these rooms."

He chuckles.

"And…" I don't know if this is the right thing to do.

"And what?"

"And your sisters..." I hesitate further, but if they live in the city, it is needed. I know I'd have done a lot of things—drastic things, even—to make a coin or two after leaving Daros—if I had cared about my life. "Make certain they are paid for their assistance."

His eyebrows shoot up. "Thank you. They will much appreciate it."

I shrug. "I don't know how much money the crown has, but it should be enough to pay those who work for her."

"There is plenty from what I recently learned. The last queen taxed heavily, and those laws are still in place."

The thought burns me. "We should do something about that, too."

His smile hides something I don't understand.

"What?" I ask.

"It's great that you're beginning to care more."

Compliments are unfamiliar beasts. Despite that, I think I like them.

"You should talk to the council about your coronation ball," Nash says. "I agree that it's a good idea, but you'll get more of them on your side by consulting them, instead of plowing them over with the news."

I don't want to, but— "You have a point. Will you set up a meeting? Or have a Head of Relations with the Queen do it?"

"Consider it done. Now, why don't we learn something about foreign relations?"

I groan. "It's a nice thought, even if I feel like my head is pounding with information."

"That's the spirit. What do you know about other countries?"

"I know they exist." My assassin jobs didn't ever take me to another country.

"It's a start."

Despite his encouraging voice, I feel like I've failed him. "I know Torhun has a King," I say. "Do you think a patriarchy or matriarchy is better?"

"Am I supposed to answer that?"

"Yes," I say, bewildered. Why wouldn't he answer that?

"It's just that it's like walking with a cliff on both sides. If I say *patriarchy*, I'm in trouble, because I'm not supporting my queen. If I say *matriarchy*, I'm in trouble because I'm not supporting my gender."

"Ah. I can see how that would be difficult."

He laughs. "Not as bad as working with the King of Torhun. I hear he's a beast. So maybe a matriarchy is better after all."

"Do I have to work with him often?"

"Your Head of Foreign relations, Mina, will do most of what needs done and then report to you. Honestly, you should know about our neighboring countries, but we have very little interaction with them."

"Good to know." And it is. That means less that I'll have to learn to catch up on.

As he continues to speak, I find that paying attention isn't so bad when I want to learn. And learn I do. Nash is a superb teacher.

If only everything else about being the queen would come a little easier.

CHAPTER 19

THE LADY *in green stands before me. "Who are you?"*

This is getting old.

"I agree. It is rather tiresome. Nevertheless, I need to know. Who are you?"

"I'm no one." Though I feel stronger than I did before.

"That's something. Still, I need you to admit who you are."

"Why does it matter?"

"It's a vital step in becoming who you were meant to be."

I shake myself. This sounds like nonsense. I know who I am, and I don't like it.

"Then admit it to me. Stop hiding it. I promise I'm here to help." Her voice is soft. Kind and caring.

Doesn't mean I need to divulge everything, though, even in my dreams. "Are you real?"

"As real as the Mortum Tura."

Which only serves to make me wonder how real the drink is. Should I really drink it a lot, like she said?

"It's up to you. I won't force you to, but it will make you stronger. The more you drink, the more power you have and the longer you live."

"It's creepy that you keep answering my thoughts."

She smiles. "I'm afraid I can't help being in your head."

"If the death drink makes one more powerful, why did the last queen die after only five years?"

"Ah, poor Deedra... She was a dear thing. I don't fully understand her death. I know she was murdered. It was a sad ending, for one so young."

"She didn't seem young."

"Well, young to me. She was in her late twenties, so older than you are. I think. I have a hard time telling your age."

I do too. It's not like I have a birthday. Seventeen years of age is more of a guess. "I still don't follow. Why do queens die early if they have the power of the Mortum Tura behind them?"

"Because people still have choices. Queens aren't always as strong as they should be. But you—you're different. Something about you makes me think you might be The One."

"What one?"

"The one to rule for a lifetime."

No. I'm having a hard enough time with it as it is. I don't want to think about doing it for longer.

I roll over and give a heavy blink.

It was only a dream. Nothing more.

CHAPTER 20

THE COUNCIL ROOM IS FULL, with the council members positioned the same way as on the day I first met them. It makes them easier to remember. Except Ranen isn't in the same spot. Instead of next to me, he sits across from me, clear at the other end of the room. The farthest from me possible. I'll take it.

Nash is on my right. His smile gives me courage.

"What have you brought us together for, Your Majesty?" Ranen snips.

"You shouldn't be questioning the Queen," Yuka says.

"I have an announcement to make." I center myself, ignoring their quips. "I would like to host a coronation ball for the people to attend, Kurah, Medi, and Poruah classes all."

To my dismay, there are scowls and mutterings. Not the response I expected.

"I don't want to be the one to break this to you"—the tone of Ranen's voice sounds as if he likes being in charge—"but we don't mingle with peasants. The queen, especially, shouldn't."

"Why not?"

"Because," Borkus, Head of Design, says, "it just isn't done."

I want to fume. "That's not good enough."

His eyebrows come together in a frown. "It's been good enough for past queens. Why not you?"

Why not, indeed? Maybe because I understand the people's plight? At least apparently more than they do. And maybe because I think it would be good for them to get to know me? Whatever the case, I say, "The people need us. We should show them that we care. That we are interested in their lives. Otherwise, one of these days, they may revolt."

"I think you're being a little dramatic, Your Majesty," Timit says.

I've had worse things said to me. Doesn't mean I like this man, though. I narrow my eyes at him.

"I, for one, think it's a good idea, Your Highness." Yuka, Head of Arts, lifts her chin.

"Thank you." At least I have the support of one person besides Nash. Still, I need more. "As for the rest of you... I need to be coronated. Why not do so in the public eye?"

"They'll be able to see her for who she is." Though well intentioned, Nash's words make me cringe. Their seeing me is the last thing I want. He continues. "They'll see she has a good heart and wants what's best for them. Who knows? Maybe she'll be able to bring Valcora together in a way that hasn't been managed before."

Now he's being too hopeful. None of that sounds like me. Not even close.

"And that way might just be the worst thing possible," Kada, Head of Relations with the queen, says. "You're right that we don't know what the people will do. They could use the ball to try to topple the government. We all know what happened last time they tried to get rid of the queen."

They all nod, but I don't have a clue. Is it common knowledge, which I don't share because I was sheltered, or is it something only the council knows? Either way, I risk looking dumb when I ask, "What happened?"

"It was before any of our time, but there are stories that say the very ground shook," Yuka says. "That tempests came and destroyed lives and homes. Ruination came upon all people of Valcora."

"When was this?" Could the stories be true?

"It was about one hundred and fifty years ago, Your Majesty," Yuka says.

Long enough that no one was around, but not so long that the truth would be twisted much. If it was the truth to begin with.

"Whatever the case may be, I don't believe we will have a revolt from the Poruah class."

"Quite the opposite," Nash says. "They should welcome the Queen's thinking of them and providing for them, even if it's for one day."

"You don't know that," Timit says. "It could be the worst thing to ever happen to this country."

"That's an exaggeration." Nash's hands are fists, but otherwise he remains calm.

"You want the world to fall apart?" Borkus asks, voice calm despite his words.

"No one said anything about the world falling apart," Yuka says. "It's a simple ball for the people to come to know their queen. To see they can trust her and her decisions."

Ranen pounds the table. "We will not mix with peasants. If we're to have a ball, at least make it with only the Kurah class."

It takes all my willpower not to jump out of my seat. "*Peasants,* as you call them, are the foundation this nation is built on."

"No one is denying that, Your Highness," Borkus says. "But there's no point in us mingling with them."

"Definitely not." Kada scowls at me.

"So we all agree the queen should be coronated at a ball only for the Kurah class," Ranen says, voice oily.

"No, we do not agree." Yuka looks ready to burst.

Ranen shoots her a glare strong enough to set her ablaze. "Those of us who matter agree."

"This coming from the Head of Furniture," Monkia, the Head of Staff, says.

It takes a great deal of control to not titter.

Ranen slams his fist down on the table again, so hard I can feel the vibrations all the way over where I'm sitting. He wrinkles his nose. "I have connections far above someone the likes of you," he tells Monkia.

"Enough." I don't want to be around Ranen's temper any longer. It's too reminiscent of Daros's. "I understand your concerns, and I appreciate you voicing them. But I am going to hold this coronation ball."

I stand, not waiting to see their reactions. Nash follows me out of the room and into the halls. Guards surround us. I recognize Afet, Wilric, and Eldim. The other two are unfamiliar to me, but this is usually the case. They switch out so often, I can't be sure who is who, except for the ones that stay by my side.

We're silent as we walk through the halls. I want to talk, but I don't want to do so in front of the guards if I can help it.

We leave the guards outside my rooms, and I plop into a chair. Nash gives me a look, like he knows I'm not being ladylike but isn't going to hassle me about it. Thank my daggers. The last thing I want right now is more etiquette lessons.

"How do you think that went?" I ask after he sits on the chair next to mine.

"You handled it well. Those against the idea will come around, but even if they don't, they're bound to have new respect for you for standing up to them. And we know Yuka is on your side."

"That's much appreciated. I'll take what I can get." I relax back into my seat. So one person. Possibly two, if Monkia is not just against Ranen, but also for my ideas.

"My sisters were excited to find out they get to help plan the ball," Nash says, changing the subject, thankfully. I'm sick of thinking about it.

"I'm glad to hear that." The thought of meeting them makes me nervous. I haven't done well with people, and for some reason, I want his sisters to like me.

"I had them meet up with the Head of Staff, and together, they're coming up with some good ideas to implement. Opening up more of the palace so we can fit extra people in it. Having everything, from basic country fare to more upscale versions, so people from all walks of life feel comfort in what they eat or excitement to try something new."

I want to choke down my fears, but they insist on coming out. "Do you really think this is going to work? Won't the Kurah class snub the Poruah class? I don't want them to feel slighted."

"If you are kind to the Poruah class, I'm sure the upper and middle classes will follow your lead. They usually emulate the queen."

"It's nerve-wracking."

He moves closer. "I know, but you're going to do great."

The warmth of his presence is more reassuring than his words.

I can only hope he's right.

CHAPTER 21

"You've barely left your rooms since becoming Queen."

Nash's words echo in my mind all through my sleepless night as well as while my servants prepare me for the day.

I don't consider myself a coward, but that one line makes me think I may be more of one than I speculated.

The thought consumes me as my servants dance around me, hurrying from one task to another. It's excessive, but I've put up with it to this point, despite them driving me nuts. They're the familiar women, though I haven't learned any of their names. I should change that, but it would make me feel as if I'm getting too close to them.

I don't want to get close to anyone. Nash already pushes my boundaries. I'm not sure I can handle anyone else.

A pin jabs my wrist. *"Ow."*

A ripple of gasps goes through the girls as I inspect the wound. Nothing major. Just surprised me.

But they all stare at me like they know my secrets. My chest seems to compress in on itself. They can't know my secrets from the little interaction they had with me. A prick of a pin wouldn't reveal them, either.

Their eyes widen, like they're horrified of what they find

within me.

"Why are you all looking at me like that?" I demand.

No one answers.

"Why?" I ask again.

A girl younger than me steps forward. Her voice quivers, but she speaks clearly. "We are waiting for you to punish the girl who pricked you or punish all of us."

"Is that what you're used to from Queen Deedra?"

The girl nods.

Me too.

"Everyone out," I say, and then point at the girl who spoke up. "Except you."

The other girls flee from the room, leaving the poor girl alone to face what they probably think to be a terrible fate.

"What is your name?" I demand.

"Inkga." Her bottom lip quivers.

"Oh, stop that. You're brave enough to speak up when no one else does. You may as well be brave enough to face me alone."

She clamps her jaw down and clasps her hands together.

"Good. How harsh was the last queen?"

The girl doesn't respond.

"Come on now. She's not here to inflict damage on you anymore. Answer me."

"I believe, Your Majesty, that she was a sad person. At first, she didn't take that out on us, but as she grew in confidence over the years she ruled, she grew in cruelty. Beheadings were common."

The thought makes me sick. "I promise that won't happen to you under my rule," I say.

"Your Highness, forgive me, but I believe every queen has gotten to that point at one time or another."

I want to rage on behalf of those innocents other queens harmed. Instead, I force out, "Not this one."

She nods, relief filling her eyes.

"Now," I say, "I have to do this in public, eventually, but I'd like you to become my Head Servant."

She gasps. "Why would you want to do that?"

"Because you're courageous—well, mostly—and you will tell me the truth."

"I don't know what to say."

"Tell me you accept the position."

"I accept the position."

"Good."

She hesitates, and then says, "What is it exactly that you want me to do?"

"For starters, these dresses are horrid."

Inkga laughs—a high, sparkling sound. "I'm glad you think so too. The last Head Servant picked them out under Borkus's tutelage. They thought they were fitting for a queen."

"Some queen, but not me."

"No. I think you'd do much better with less lacy and more sleek."

"I'm already glad I upgraded your position."

"A redone wardrobe. That's simple," she says. "What else can I do to please you?"

"Pants. Clothes with lots of places to stash weapons. And less servants would be good. All this prancing about me drives me mad."

"It's not technically my job, but I'll pass the word onto the Head of Staff and make sure she gets it done. Anything else?"

"I'll let you know when there is." I'm surprised she said nothing about my need to stash weapons. The seamstresses had better do a good job of it.

"I will go get started on your new wardrobe, my lady." She curtsies and hurries toward the door.

"Inkga," I force myself to say the next words before she leaves to go to her duties, "thank you for accepting this new position."

She almost smiles. "Of course." With another curtsy, she's gone.

One less thing for me to worry about. Though I fear there are a lot more important things on my plate I'm not as certain about how to handle.

CHAPTER 22

NASH IS DRILLING me on the government officials and laws and has been for three hours. I'm getting a headache.

"Did you know it's a law that only women can ask for a man's hand in marriage?"

That gets my attention. "I thought that was only custom."

"Nope. It's law."

I should fix that one.

"You don't seem to know a lot about common law."

I shrug.

"Were you aware that it's a death sentence if you don't pay your taxes?"

"I wasn't." No clue at all. It explains why so many people go hungry, choosing a slow death instead of a quick one by the state.

"It's caused a lot of heated debate, but the last queen was positive she wanted it that way, no matter what anyone said."

"She sounds like a tyrant."

A knock sounds. Nash answers it and turns to me. "Your ladies in waiting have requested an audience."

Just what I don't want on top of these lessons. I wave my hand. "Tell them to come back later."

He lifts an eyebrow but doesn't comment. After turning them

away, he returns to his chair. "Moving on," he says. "Taxes must be paid in coin. No animal or crops allowed. Taxes are collected once a week. Taxes are to be paid to the tax collector without delay. Tax collectors aren't to be harmed on pain of death."

The list goes on and on, most of it sounding the same as previous laws. There must be a reason for having so many, but I find it hard to care.

"Are you listening?" Nash asks, voice patient and kind.

"Who ruled when the last queen died?"

"I'll take that as a *no*."

I give him a look.

With a sigh, he says, "Ranen. The Head Advisor always rules between queens."

Is that why he's so power hungry? He was basically doing my job not that long ago. "Does that mean you'll rule when I'm dead?"

"It does." His mouth is tight.

"How does that make you feel?" I find myself really wanting to know.

"It doesn't matter."

"It matters to me. Tell me."

"Fine. It scares me, if you must know. I'm having a hard time guiding you. I don't know what I'd do if I had to lead. Another reason for you to stay alive."

Hmm. "I've put you in a difficult position."

"It's all right."

"I could find someone else to be Head Advisor. Not Ranen, but someone."

"Why not Ranen? He's well connected and has a lot of experience."

"I don't trust him."

"Why not?"

So many reasons. "Do you trust him?"

"No."

Good. "Probably for the same reasons as you, then. Something about him gives me pause and makes me wonder what he's up to.

I want him where he can do the least amount of damage, but where I can still keep an eye on him."

"That's why you put him in charge over furniture?"

"It is." Part of the reason, anyway.

He gives a ghost of a smile. "It makes a lot more sense now. But we've gotten off track. We should talk more about the laws you need to know."

I huff and pop out of my chair. "If we're going to continue this, can we get a change of scenery? I'm sick of this room. It's too confining."

"I'm glad you're taking an interest in more than what's in here."

"Any person would go mad, spending all this time in a room."

"It's true, and we will go out, but not yet."

"What do you mean *not yet*?" I demand.

"Well, we could go out, but this is stuff you need to know. You can't be seen going over the government officials in the gardens. You should know them by now. Not knowing them will make you seem weak. And..." He hesitates.

"And weakness will get me killed." I roll my eyes. "Like anyone could kill me if they tried."

"Want to put a wager on that?"

I try not to grin. "Wager on what, exactly?"

"We fight. I win—we continue lessons on government. You win —we go outside and pretend you have no responsibilities."

"Problem is, if I win, you'll be dead."

He shakes his head, giving a little laugh like he doesn't think I'm serious. "We're not playing until someone dies."

"Or you'll be in a coma."

He lets out a huff. "No killing and no putting people in a coma."

"Then how will we know when someone wins?"

He shakes his head with a chuckle. "When the other person gives up."

"Then I've already won," I say. "I never give up." Neither of us mentions that we're not supposed to touch.

He smiles, like he has no idea how serious I am. Like he has no idea how much torture I've been through to get where I am. "We'll see."

"Fine, then. We play until the other person gives up." I pull out a regular old dagger to start with. I may as well go easy on him at first.

"Whoa. No weapons," he says.

"Don't worry, this isn't my poisoned dagger."

"You have a poisoned dagger?" He shakes his head. "That's probably not the safest idea."

"Whyever not?"

"What if you scratch yourself on accident?"

"I don't have accidents. Besides, I've built up an immunity to this type of poison."

He gives me a look. "What would make you do that?"

"I can't tell you my secrets."

"You are something else. You know that?" He gives me a look that heats me through.

I smile. "I'll take that as a compliment."

"But seriously, no weapons."

My smile fades as I put my dagger back in its hiding place through my skirt pocket. I wonder what the laundress thinks of all the cutting I'm doing to my clothes, for pockets to stash my sheathed daggers in. "Isn't this a little unfair?" I ask.

"You agreed to the terms. Unless you want to back out now, and we can continue with our lesson."

"I meant unfair to you."

He laughs—a big sound that makes my chest feel warm. "I'm not worried about me."

"Let's go for this, then." I start pushing the furniture aside. The one bad thing about comfy chairs is they tend to weigh more than torturous ones.

"Here?" he asks.

"Might as well. I'm eager to begin, and it's big."

Nash helps, and together we clear a space in the middle of the room.

"It's probably a little unfair that you're wearing skirts," he says, loosening up his muscles on the other side of the room.

"Maybe, but I think it's not enough to even the odds between us." I stretch my arms, warming them up.

"You're quite sure of yourself, aren't you?"

"I have to be."

"Because you are the queen?"

"Because of my secrets."

He cocks his head to one side, like he's studying me. "Maybe someday you'll feel like sharing a secret or two with me."

"And maybe someday you'll feel like letting my secrets be."

"I wouldn't count on it."

"And I wouldn't count on my telling you any of them."

"Fair enough."

"For now."

His lips twitch like he's trying not to smile again. "Are you ready to start this?"

"Only if you are."

"Let's go, then." He crouches down and slowly comes toward me.

I let him come closer, not making a move.

"Are you going to try?" he asks.

"I'm letting you do the hard work."

He chuckles. Next thing I know, he's at my side, arms around my waist, pulling me down. I let myself sink to the floor, and then I buck up my legs to kick him in the chest. First injury is mine. I've already won this fight.

He grunts. "Take those high heels off. They're as bad as a weapon."

As he rubs his chest where I kicked him, I take off my shoes and throw them by the furniture.

He comes at me again.

I can't help but grin.

I bend and wrap my arms around his upper thigh, then yank as hard as I can. He topples to the carpet, bringing me down with him. Though I want to punch him in the face, I refrain because it's

JANEAL FALOR

him. Instead, I plop my butt on the ground with my legs wrapped around his arm and bend it backwards. He tries to kick up at my head, but I lean away from his attacks.

I forgot how much fun this is.

Next thing I know, he's got me pinned beneath him. It's more fun than I first thought. He won't expect me to beat him now, but this is perfect.

We grapple for a moment. I don't want him to feel totally humiliated, just enough to keep him from winning. Plus, there's something nice about being this close to him. It has my heart racing with more than exertion.

He tries to hold me still, as I squirm. Sometimes I let him, pretending I can't move. Other times, I wiggle out and let him capture me again.

Once I feel like he's gotten a good show in, I squirm my way out of the hold easily, twist around, and jump on his back.

He stands. I grip his throat and wrap my legs around his waist, locking one foot behind my other knee.

He tries to pry me loose, but I won't be moved without a weapon. I've had much practice at this. Besides, touching him is thrilling. It gives me pleasant tingles up and down my skin. That in and of itself is reason to hold on.

It's no surprise when he tries to shake me off, and even less of one when he falls backward, making me slam into the ground.

As I catch my breath, I focus on grasping tight. "You're not worried about hurting the queen?"

"Not anymore," he gasps out.

I squeeze him as tight as I can, with both my arms and legs. No way he's getting out of this. He tries, holding out longer than I expect. He should be about ready to pass out any second.

"You concede?" I ask, letting triumph color my words.

"Yes," he gasps.

I let him go, thrilled with my victory. I'm done with lessons for a while. It's definitely time for something else. Though I do miss the contact.

"You fight hard," Nash says, still catching his breath.

"I was going easy on you." I contemplate going after my shoes, but I like this barefoot feeling much better. In fact, I like the furniture pushed back as well.

"You're kidding, right?" he asks.

"Why would I joke about something like fighting? I always take it seriously."

He shakes his head. "No wonder you took out the men who tried to kill you. How do you know how to fight so well?"

I shrug. "Just do."

He narrows his eyes at me like he's trying to discover more about me.

"Now to the gardens?" I eagerly stand by the door.

He laughs and rubs his chest. "Now to the gardens."

CHAPTER 23

THE GARDENS ARE full of every plant I could ever imagine and more that I couldn't. A blossom of nature's magic. They're wild and overgrown in a beautiful way, but have still been cut back to allow for paths and benches. Not only are they gorgeous, but they're huge with fountains and miniature waterfalls.

"It's lovely here," I say.

"They'd be lovelier if I wasn't in such pain," Nash replies.

"You're the one who wanted to fight."

He grimaces. "True."

"Why did you suggest it?" I ask.

He gives a humorless laugh. "You always go on about how you can take care of yourself. I thought it would be my chance to show you that you need me and get you to agree to learn more about the government."

"And what do you think now?"

"You can take care of yourself," he says, "but you still need guards for when you're sleeping and so people don't know how tough you really are. You can use that to your advantage."

"I know." I give him a wide grin.

He shakes his head. "The lessons can't end permanently, though."

I sigh. "I know that too."

"Good."

We walk silently for several minutes. The sound of birds' twitters fills the air. It's a refreshing break from the daily grind.

"What do you do when you're not working for me?" I ask.

"I'm pretty much always working for you."

I know what that's like—always working for someone. "Would you like that to change?" I hope the answer is *no*.

He shrugs. "I don't know. I haven't given it much thought."

"Give some thought to it now."

It takes him a minute to respond. "It would be nice to see my family more."

"Why don't we move your family into the palace?"

"It's kind of you to offer, but my mother would hate it. Besides, in case you haven't noticed, this is a dangerous place to live."

"And yet you want to continue to stay here," I say, hoping it's true.

"I can hold my own." He laughs. "Or I thought I could, before you whipped me."

"There are things I can teach you if you'd like."

"That's the nicest thing you've ever said to me."

"Can I take that as a *yes*?" I ask, tickled at the words he spoke.

"A definite *yes*."

The thought of my teaching him something for a change is welcome. What's more is the thought of being that close to him—of touching him when I need to correct his position, or showing him a certain move. It has me feeling hot and blushing for reasons I don't understand.

"Tell me about your family," Nash says.

The hot feeling evaporates. "I have none."

"Everyone has to have parents at some point. What happened to yours?"

My chest grows tight. "I don't know. I was abandoned when I was a baby." I haven't told anyone that before. What made me tell him?

"I know it doesn't make a difference, but I'm sorry."

I shrug. "It happened before I can remember, so it's all the same to me."

The garden is a good distraction. The flowers are so pretty. We turn the corner and find Faya and Borkus strolling together. He's wearing a sky-blue jacket with lots of lace and froo froo. It almost hurts to look at. Faya is a lot more stately, in a deep-maroon gown, though she has wider skirts and more lace than I care for. She holds herself stiff and apart from him. I don't blame her.

They grow closer to us. When they're within speaking distance, they stop, and Borkus bows while Faya curtsies.

"You may stand," I say. The words feel so silly coming out of my mouth. Like they don't belong to me.

"What brings you out today?" Nash asks them.

"Borkus and I were discussing the latest trends of the Kurah class," Faya says.

How exciting.

"Yes. We think there are some wonderful trends out there. Don't you think, Your Majesty?" Borkus preens.

I open my mouth when Nash ever so gently nudges my foot with his. A quick glance at him reveals nothing. His face is clean of expression, but I know what he wants of me—to interact and not be rude about it. I suppress a sigh. "Honestly, I haven't noticed."

"Of course she hasn't." Ranen rounds the corner.

What is it about this man that makes me want to vomit? I stand with my back to a hedge, trying to watch him and the other two at the same time. I don't trust anyone. I don't even like turning my back to Nash, if I'm truthful with myself.

"You have to remember our queen hasn't been out much since coming to court." Ranen's voice holds a hint of a sneer, but to his credit, he does bow—a stiff, jerky thing. He doesn't wait for permission to rise.

"I hope the trends go to what I like. There's too much fluff around here." I try to soften my words with a smile but don't know if I succeed.

Borkus coughs. "Your tastes are certainly… different."

"I, for one, think Your Majesty has wonderful taste. I could do with a little less." Faya motions to her wide skirt and lace.

I grin at her. "My servant, Inkga, is having some made special for me. Perhaps she knows someone who could help you."

"That's a very kind offer, Your Majesty. I do believe I'm familiar with Inkga. I will ask her myself."

"Perfect." I'm not the only one who wants simple things.

"Yes. Perfect," Ranen says dryly. "As to matters of state, I wonder if you have considered letting me be an assistant advisor. Nash is very capable, but you would do well under my tutelage."

I feel Nash staring holes into me. Because of that, I temper my response. "Thank you for the offer, but I currently need no other assistance."

Ranen tenses his jaw. When I glance at Nash, he's barely suppressing the upward curl of his lips.

"We, on the council, do a great job at guiding you, eh?" Borkus chuckles.

I don't see anything funny.

"The council is a great asset to the queen," Nash says, "as are her ladies in waiting."

Not that I talk to either. I appreciate his support, though.

"As stimulating as this conversation is, some of us have work to do." Ranen gives another stiff bow and takes off back the way he came.

I watch him until he disappears from sight.

"I must be going as well," Faya says. "It was a pleasure to bump into you, Your Highness."

"And I will follow after you," Borkus says.

They both bow before passing by Nash and me and following Ranen.

Once they're out of sight, I whisper, "That was quite the meeting."

Nash and I continue walking. His strides match my own, quicker now than before.

"You don't like talking of clothes and frivolities?" he asks.

I snort. Thankfully, he lets it pass. "The gardens are a busy place today," I say.

"So it would seem."

"Thank you for having my back."

He glances at me. "I will always have your back."

The warmth from earlier returns, even if I'm not ready to leave myself unguarded.

CHAPTER 24

BARELY ANYTHING HAPPENS *before the lady in green says, "You've been avoiding me."*

Easy answer to that. "Don't talk about things I don't want to discuss, and we won't have that problem."

"We have so much work to do." She sighs. "All is well. I'm here for you, whenever you need me. Now, let us begin. Who are you?"

I hesitate. Am I ready to say this? Whether I am or not, it's true. "I am the queen."

She smiles at me and puts a hand on my shoulder. "You are, as am I."

"You?"

"Yes. I am the first queen."

"The first? Ever?"

"For Valcora, yes," she says.

"How can this be?"

"From the Mortum Tura. You didn't think the only thing it did was make you queen, did you?"

"I never thought about it." What else does it do? Or do I now know all?

"That's why I'm here. To help you with thinking about things you need to. Things that will help you rule."

"What's your name?"

"*You can call me* Queen."

It's weird that, when I finally accept that's who I am, I find someone else who is as well.

"*Now, are you ready to tell me who Daros is?" she asks. It feels like she's trying to tap into my mind. To chip away at my mental defenses.*

"*Not likely," I say.*

"*Fine, then. We'll do things the long way. Eventually you will tell me, you know."*

I cross my arms. "*We'll see."*

"*A queen doesn't cross her arms like that. It gives away her emotions."*

I don't uncross them. "*What if I want to give my emotions away?"*

"*Then I suppose it's acceptable."*

"*Is that what I'm coming here for? To learn more about the things everyone in real life is trying to teach me?"*

Her face softens. "*No. I mean, yes, there will be some of that. I will help you in any way I can, but that's not why I left a part of myself behind."*

"*Why did you? And how?"*

"*The how isn't important yet. Right now, you need to know why," she says. "When I made the cup the way it was, I knew it would draw a lot of women."*

"*Wait. You made the cup?"*

"*I did. I needed a way to help those who become queen. You see, the cup is made special so that only those who don't want the power of being a queen can become one."*

"*So it would have only killed me if I didn't want it to?" The thought stuns me.*

"*Correct. I had to leave something behind to guide you because I knew only girls who would be in a vulnerable place would become queens."*

"*Why would you want that?" I ask, still at a loss.*

"*Because those who want to become queen are power hungry. They don't want what's best for the country; they want what's best for themselves. They want to be able to say they rule over all. It's not what I wanted for my country."*

"I can understand that." I know all about power-hungry people. *"But isn't killing the rest of the girls going too far?"*

She sighs. *"I regret that it had to be so. There was no other way for me to make the cup. It had to be done like this or not at all."*

I don't understand magic. It's as brutal as Daros.

She lifts her eyebrows, and I clamp down all thoughts of Daros.

She purses her lips. *"I'm getting off course. I knew when I designed the cup that it would create queens who would not necessarily want to live. Some didn't want to die, but only took the Mortum Tura because of family or friends pressuring them into taking it. But you're not the first to feel your life wasn't worth living."*

"If you knew why, you'd agree with me."

"It's very strange that I can't see the reason. You bury it deep. Please tell me. I can help you work through this, but it starts with talking."

"I can't."

I bolt awake. To my surprise, tears wet my cheeks.

CHAPTER 25

INKGA IS READYING me for the day. My new clothes haven't been made yet, but she's made a few alterations to the ones I own, so I don't have to go around in quite as much lace and fluff. Plus I have easier access to my weapons.

"Do you know how the plans for the ball are coming along?" I ask, pushing away thoughts of the first queen trying to find out why my life is no longer worth living.

"It should be quite the event. I don't think the people have seen anything like it in their lifetime."

"Good." As I want it to be.

"There." She does the last button. I'll be glad when they're all where I can reach them once again. "There's someone who wants to see you as soon as you're finished."

"Oh?"

"Your lady in waiting, Jem."

I want to grind my teeth at the thought of her, but I refrain myself. "What does she want?"

"I'm not certain."

Wonderful.

"That will be all," I say, moving to my sitting room while Inkga follows me. "You may send her in as you leave."

"Yes, Your Highness." With a bow, she leaves the room.

I take a seat on the comfiest of chairs. Despite that, I don't feel comfortable. I feel...something. That talk with the first queen has me on edge. I wonder if anyone has ever heard of her before, besides previous queens who I can't speak with. I feel like she can be trusted—like she really can help—but I'm not ready to open up.

There's a knock on the door. I wish it was Nash.

"Enter," I call out.

In sways Jem, and she closes the door behind her. She gives me a curtsy, and I motion her up. As much as I'd like to keep her in suspense, it's too awkward.

"Sit," I say.

She takes the chair across from mine. "Thank you for seeing me, Your Majesty."

I hold back a grunt. "What do you need?"

She takes a deep breath. If I didn't know better, I'd say it was shaky. "It's about the ball."

Of course it is. I give her a *keep-talking* look.

"The other ladies in waiting and I want to be more involved."

"I'm not the person to ask about that."

She crinkles her eyebrows. "But you are the queen."

"Things are different now than when my predecessor was here." I should make them even more different. It's time I tackle the laws and find a way to feed the Poruah class. If the Kurah class can make a feast for me, surely there's a way we can achieve that.

"Maybe things shouldn't be different." Jem startles me out of my thoughts.

"You dare disagree with me?"

She straightens her back and stares me down in a way that makes me think she's ready to start a fight. "Ladies in waiting have an important part too."

"If you mean not getting tested to become queen and wanting to get rid of me so you can do so, then it's not so important."

She stands, face going red. "Taking your life didn't cross my mind. If you would stop being so self-centered you'd see there's a lot we have to offer."

Her words sting with truth. "You have nothing to offer me."

"Fine. But don't come crying to me when you can't do every-thing and you need help. We won't be there to give it to you," she says and storms from the room.

Why do I have a feeling I made a horrible mistake?

I stay up late thinking. As much as I don't want to admit it, maybe Jem was right. When I finally go to sleep, there are no dreams. No nightmares. No lady in green.

CHAPTER 26

IN THE MORNING, I finish getting ready and dismiss my servants.

There's a knock on my sitting room door.

"Come in," I say.

Nash enters with a bow. He shuts the door and picks a chair.

"How are you this morning?" he asks.

"Well enough. You?"

"Charmed to be in your presence."

My cheeks heat. "Now you're trying to flatter me."

"Get used to it. It will happen often while you're the queen."

"Is that why you said it?" I ask.

"Um...Precisely." He glances away from me. "Should we get on with our lesson?"

I'd rather wrestle with him more. "Fine."

He starts with his lecture for the day, but I only give half an ear. I should pay attention, but Jem's visit yesterday has me unsure of what to do. It's difficult to think of much else. It's occupied my thoughts all morning.

Does she want to help me, or does she want to see me fail so she can have a chance at being the queen? She'd also have a large chance at dying, but maybe it'd be worth it to her. It seems worth it to so many people.

What about the other ladies in waiting? What are they after? There's no way to know for certain if I don't give them a chance. Is there a way I can use them without risking anything? Perhaps.

"Have the ladies in waiting help with the ball," I tell Nash.

"Where's this coming from?" he asks. "I thought you stayed away from them as much as possible."

"What gave you that idea?"

"The fact that you didn't want anything to do with them. You never invite them in like the other queens did. They'd spend an hour with them every day. Though they weren't the same ones you have, she listened to their advice as much as to the Head Advisor's."

"You want me to listen to someone's advice besides your own? Someone who might want me dead?"

"That's not what I'm saying, though I don't think it's bad to get more than one person's perspective on things."

I shrug. "I don't want to be best friends with them, just have them help with the ball."

"Well, it will be a good thing. My sisters are doing a great job with it so far, but more hands would make it easier."

"Good."

What else do we need to talk about? *The dreams.* Should I tell him they're happening? Something in me curls away from that idea. I don't want to sound more insane than he already thinks I am.

Still, I want to know more about them. To understand them. How can I get that information?

"Tell me if you know anything about the first queen of Valcora," I say.

"That's a different question than what we usually cover."

I shrug.

"Don't get me wrong—I think history is important, but this seems out of nowhere. You're surprising me today."

"Just keeping you on your toes."

He smiles, and something about that smile makes me want to move closer.

Instead, I clear my throat. "So do you know anything?"

"Honestly, I should know a lot more about history than I do, but I didn't go to school." That's no surprise; only the wealthiest can afford to send their children. "There's bound to be information around the palace library if you're interested in learning something, though. I don't know how much they'll have about the first queen, since she reigned so long ago, but there should be at least something."

"I'll keep that in mind."

He leans closer. "What's this all about?"

"What do you mean?"

"You seem different. Like there's something else going on that you're not telling me."

I contemplate speaking with him about my dreams, but what would I say? It's not like magic is common; it's a distant myth, barely spoken of. He might believe me, but do I want him to know? Until I'm sure, I can't do it. "There's lots I don't tell you."

"I really wish you would. It would be helpful to us both."

"So you keep saying."

He mutters something.

"What was that?"

He opens his mouth and then stops himself. "You know, I don't have to tell you unless you order me to. You're not the only one who can keep secrets."

"At least I don't do it out of spite."

He huffs. "You're right. I shouldn't keep secrets just because I'm upset with you. But that doesn't mean you're going to like what you'll hear."

"Tell me anyway. I can handle it." Can't be much, compared to what I'm used to handling.

"Fine. I hate that you don't share things with me. I hate this stubborn trait you have. It's all right to keep things close sometimes, but you keep everything close. You don't tell anyone anything. How is that helpful?"

"It's not. Maybe that's the point."

He stands, walks over to the window, and leans outside. "Don't you have any feelings? Doesn't anything affect you?"

His words do, more than I want to admit. Right down to my very core. But what good would saying so do? "I appreciate your opinion."

"My opinion?" He laughs—a semi-hysterical sound. *"My opinion?* Come on. There have to be more feelings in you than that. Please, open up to me."

I bite my lip. Feelings weren't allowed at Daros's. Just because I'm not there anymore doesn't mean I'm suddenly able to. Perhaps it should, but I don't know how. "I'm afraid I can't do that."

"Well, then I'm afraid I can't stay in this room any longer. I can't be held liable for what else I might say." He gives me a final glance before clenching his jaw and leaving the room.

Even knowing secrets are meant to be kept, I wish I could have shared some emotion or thought with him.

CHAPTER 27

"YOUR NEW CLOTHES HAVE ARRIVED, Your Majesty," Inkga says when I enter my sitting room. "You should try them on, or look at them, to make certain they're what you want."

"That's fine." I don't want to look at clothes, but I'd rather make sure I'm not stuck with more lace and layers.

"Wonderful. And the kitchen sent up a tray for you while we work."

She leads me into the bedroom, where clothes are laid out on the bed. A tray of snacks and a cup sits on the vanity.

"They didn't send anything for you," I say.

She looks down, her cheeks turning red. "It's not proper for me to eat in your presence."

"Fiddlesticks. Send for another tray, same as this one. I refuse to take a bite from it until you do so."

She curtsies. "As my Queen wishes."

She goes into the sitting room, opens the door, and talks to someone I can't see. The gowns, tunics, and pants one the bed call to my attention. They are simple, like I wanted. Even the most elaborate gown among them is a far cry from the dresses they've been tying me into.

Inkga's feet pad against the carpet as she returns. "Do you like them?"

"What I've seen so far, yes. I do."

"Why don't you try some on? Then you'll be able to really tell if you like them or not."

"I am aching to get out of this dress." I'd been strapped in the layered monstrosity since this morning.

She hums an unfamiliar tune as she moves to the bed. "Which one would you like to try first?"

I pick the simplest outfit. Black pants with a blue dress and matching belt, with spots for my daggers. I prefer to keep them hidden, but this will do. There's no point in keeping them hidden now people know I defend my own life.

Not that I want them to make the connection that I'm an assassin. The last thing I want is for anyone to know what I've done.

"My Lady," Inkga says, interrupting my thoughts, "would you like to try this outfit on?" She points to the one I was contemplating.

"Yes. Help me take off this gown." I wish I could do it myself, but it's impossible with the multitude of buttons in the back.

I move in front of the mirror and turn around so I can watch while she undoes the buttons. I'm not worried that she'll want to take my life. She seems nice, but even those who seem kind have hidden agendas. She could want any number of things that don't have to do with my death.

"How have your meetings been going, Your Majesty?" she asks.

"Still learning things about the government. I didn't realize there was so much to it."

She removes the top dress and starts in on the next layer. "There is a lot, and I don't understand a fraction of it."

I keep silent as she finishes undressing me. She pulls up the tunic.

"I can get this part myself." I snatch it from her hands.

"But, Your Majesty, how am I going to be of service if I don't help you dress." She twists her hands together.

"I'm certain you can find ways to make yourself useful." I slip on the blue dress that is high on my neck with a decorated "V." It comes to my knees. I place on a double brown belt across my waist. It has a strap that goes over one shoulder as well. A fourth belt is slung across my hips with a sheath. I place some of my daggers in the belt. My dress is short enough I can reach the daggers strapped to my thighs. This is great. "Who designed this?"

"I helped our lead seamstress with it."

"You did?" I raise my eyebrows at her.

She blushes. "Yes."

I glance in the mirror. The outfit is striking. What I described I wanted and more. I don't know how to tell her that, though. The words want to come to my lips, but I fall awkwardly silent.

I'm saved by a knock on the sitting room door. Inkga answers it and comes back with a tray. She sets it on the vanity next to the other one.

"Let's drink to my new outfits," I say.

"But you haven't seen them all."

"If they're anything like this, I'm more than pleased with them." I pick up the closest cup.

After hesitating but a moment, Inkga raises the other.

"To a wonderful new wardrobe." One that will make it much easier to climb out of my rooms whenever I want. And to keep weapons on me at all times. I put my cup to my lips. As I'm about to drink, I smell something metallic.

I react before I know what I'm doing. I drop my glass and smack Inkga's away from her face. She wrinkles her eyebrows at me. "Is there something wrong, My Queen?"

"My drink was poisoned, I wasn't sure if yours was as well. Did you drink any?" I bend down to pick up the cup. There are remnants of the liquid in it.

"I did." Her face is deathly pale.

Hoping she's so white because of my words, I lift the cup to my nose and take a good whiff. Poisoned, like mine.

"Sit," I say as I scramble for the packet of poisons I keep on me at all times. Usually I use them to dress up my daggers, but there are also a couple of antidotes in there.

Inkga slumps over and falls to the floor before I can catch her. *Blast.*

"*Guards,*" I yell.

I keep my movements sure and steady as I reach for the pouch hanging about my neck like a necklace. The door to the sitting room bursts open, and Wilric and another guard I don't recognize crash into my room, swords drawn.

"She's been poisoned, though I'm certain it was meant for me." As I talk, I loosen the strings of the pouch and rummage around until I find the right antidote. "I'm in no immediate danger, but I want you to question who made these trays of food."

I force the antidote into Inkga's mouth and roll her onto her back to help her swallow it. I watch her throat as Wilric says, "We can't leave you when your life might be in danger."

"I can take care of myself," I say.

"Yes, Your Highness, but I insist on staying with you."

"Then send the other guard."

Inkga finally swallows. Did I get it to her in time? It's a brutal, quick-working poison. I roll her onto her side. "Get me—"

Before I can finish, she vomits all over my new pants. Better that than her dying.

"Too late. Go find the culprit before they escape," I say when the guards continue to stare at me. "And send a healer."

The guard I don't recognize runs from the room. Thankfully. Inkga heaves again. Wilric keeps glancing about the room, his sword at the ready. Despite not trusting him, part of me does feel safer, though I keep my wits about me.

Inkga's eyes flutter. A tension I didn't know was there falls out of me.

"What happened?" Her words are slurred.

"You were poisoned."

She groans. Having been poisoned by Daros with this exact same one, I know how she feels. It's a venom I never built an immunity to because it's not possible to do so. And you must work quickly against it if you're to live. Daros said I had to know what it was like when I failed to kill my first rat.

I shove the unbidden thoughts away. They'll do no good now.

I grab the closest piece of cloth from my bed, not caring that it's one of my new tunics, and help clean Inkga up with it. She groans again.

"I need some untainted water for her to drink." I cup the back of her head.

"Sorry, Your Majesty, but I can't leave you," Wilric says.

I huff. "Surely you don't want Inkga to die."

"Of course not, but I can't leave you either."

Thankfully, a servant comes running in. "What's happened?"

"Bring me a glass of water. Make sure you get it fresh from the tap and hurry as fast as you can," I say hoping she's trustworthy. I have no other choice.

She scurries from the room.

"How are you feeling?" I ask Inkga.

She moans.

"It's going to get better." I hope.

After a moment, she leans over and vomits again until she's dry heaving. I wish I knew more of how to help her. I only know the basics of healing.

A woman strides in the room. "What am I needed for?"

"Who are you?" Can't be too careful. I haven't seen her before.

"I'm the healer, Your Majesty."

"This woman has been poisoned with Argula. I've administered the antidote, and a servant is bringing water."

The healer's eyes grow wide. "How did you have the antidote?"

I scowl. "There are more important things going on."

"Of course, Your Highness." She hurries over and takes my position in front of Inkga, comforting her better than I could through her dry heaving.

I step back, watching the scene while still keeping an eye on my surroundings. Moments later, the servant returns with a glass of water. The healer directs Inkga to drink it, only to have it come back up again.

"More water," the healer barks at the servant.

Confident the situation is under control and that Inkga will live after going through a tough couple of hours, I head out of the room. Wilric follows close at my heel. Before we get very far, the guard who left to check on things comes running up the hallway, his face pale and Nash at his side.

When he gets to us, I ask, "What is it?"

Nash looks me over, but stays silent.

"Your Majesty." The guard bows. "I'm afraid the culprit is dead."

"What?" How can that be?

"He killed himself before we could get to him."

"How?"

"He hung himself in his room. His roommate found him moments ago after he disappeared from the kitchens."

I narrow my eyes. "And how do you know he was the culprit?"

"He left this note." He hands me a parchment with a bow.

I read it, struggling through the words and sloppy penmanship.

I REFUSE to live under such a queen. With her dead, someone new and better can reign. Tell my family I love them.

I THRUST the note back at the guard trying not to think of the words about me. "See to it his family gets this."

"I'm glad you're safe, My Queen," Nash says.

I give him a curt nod, and I storm back to my room to check on Inkga. Even knowing she'll be fine, I can't help but worry about her. I worry about myself too. I want to know who's coming after me. Mostly, though, I hate that Inkga's life was put at risk because of me.

CHAPTER 28

THE PALACE SEEMS SMALLER than when I first came. It's still huge, but less of a maze and more of a giant building. I wander through it as my guards follow until I come to a new room. A library. Perfect. Just the place to learn about the first queen.

I point at the entrance. "Stay here," I say to my guards, Eldim and a familiar woman I don't know the name of.

"Let me make certain it's safe first, My Lady," Eldim says.

"I'm perfectly safe going in myself." I make my words crisp.

"But I must insist on checking it first."

Hmm. No coward then. Plus, Inkga was poisoned. It doesn't hurt to have someone else look. Unless it's a trap he's setting up. I can handle myself if it is, though, and if it will appease him... "Very well. But make it quick."

It only takes him a minute to comb through the library and return. "The room is empty. There are still windows that could be used for an attack, though. I think it best that we remain with you."

"You will remain here." I leave them without another word. There's bravery, and then there's just plain being annoying.

The library smells very old. Musty, and like books. I savor the scent I've not had many chances to come across but always associated with happy memories. I may have found a new place to hide out if I can get away from learning things long enough.

I wish Nash was here to tell me more about the library since the librarian desk is empty. Sometimes I forget he used to only be a guard. Maybe he knows nothing of this place. I'll have to remember to ask him next time I see him. If we can get over the fight we just had, that is.

I run my hands across the books at my height, though the shelves fill the walls all the way to the ceiling. There's a ladder to reach the top books, but I go around it. What secrets do these books hold? Is there anything like mine? Or are they common knowledge to everyone but me?

I know so little about this country I'm the leader of. It wasn't in my training. Nothing was, except imitating, obeying, and killing. Perhaps becoming a shadow too. I learned plenty of things, but not outside of what Daros wanted me to know.

I move through books and books and more books, searching the titles for... I don't know what. Something about a history of the country. Perhaps the founding of Valcora. Anything that would hint at the first queen.

I come across a section of books that deal with the history of this land. I wonder if any of them contain information on the Mortum Tura and its chalice. Where it came from? How it works? Information to back up what the first queen told me, if she is the first queen.

Though if the answer was in a book, I suppose it would already be known. If someone read it. Maybe it's here and it hasn't been read in so long, everyone forgot it. I hope for the latter.

I skim through book after book, wishing reading came to me more easily. It would make this process go a lot faster.

I find nothing useful. A book on how all of Valcora is in a large valley. How pure mountain water gets to Valcora's lands. When the last invasion was—which I glance at, to find it was over five hundred years ago, when this book was written. It doesn't tell me about the first queen, though.

More books fly through my hands. *History of Economics*. *History of Farming*. The history of our language. More and more books, but nothing that looks just right.

Then I find an old, tattered book. Something the likes of which is unlike anything else around it. I'm afraid I'm going to break it just by opening it, but I do so anyway. There's no reward without taking a chance.

Inside, the very first thing I see is a picture of her. The First Queen. She's not as crisp as she is in my dreams, but it's definitely her. Even the green dress is the same.

She's real then.

And with the fact that I haven't seen this image before makes it all the more real. It's numbing. Terrifying. All too real.

But I must press on.

I search the text before and after her picture, hoping to find something that will tell me more about her. Let me know her name. Something. But there's nothing there. Nothing at all.

Instead, the book talks about the forming of Valcora. How travelers came long ago from some distance and found this land that was shielded by the mountains and decided to make it their home. It speaks of them and what they were like. How they struggled to make the land into a country they could live in. That their families could belong to.

"There you are," Ranen says, walking into the library as if he owns the place, startling me from the book.

"I see you haven't gotten to this room yet. These chairs are horrid." Not that I really care, it's just the first thing that comes to mind when I spot them.

"If I'd have known the Queen has a perchance for reading, I'd have covered this room sooner."

"I'm certain you'll remedy that."

"Yes, whatever I can do to help my Queen." Though the words are fine, the way he says them like he not only thinks me a child but wants me out of his way leaves me feeling like pulling out my poisoned dagger. I don't even know why.

"What is it you want?"

"I just wanted to check in and see how my work is going for you. Clearly there's more room for improvement, but I'd like to think I'm making it to your liking."

I shrug. "What work you have done is fine."

"I thought then perhaps we could speak about a change of position. Or even having me work as the Furniture Master while I'm also assisting you in another way. You'll find I'm capable of taking a lot on. I have a lot to offer you as Head Advisor."

"That may be, but I have no further use for you than as a Furniture Master."

"My skills are much more suited to something else."

I narrow my eyes at him. "I know what your skills are good for." Scheming.

He takes a step closer. Slowly, I reach for one of my daggers. All my senses are on alert, but I try to keep him from realizing it. I don't think he'll do anything to me; he's too sniveling for that. That doesn't mean he won't have someone else stab me in the back while he has my attention, though.

"You know nothing about me."

"I know enough."

He bares his teeth at me. "You don't understand who I am. What I can do to you."

"Is that a threat?"

"Of course not, Your Majesty," he spits out. "I wouldn't threaten you."

"Good, because I can get rid of you any time I want."

"You will not get rid of me. I have powerful people on my side." His voice is low, but ominous.

I mimic his tone. "I will do what I want to do."

"Then you will have consequences of my choosing." As loud as he is, I expect the guards to come running in, but they don't.

I can do without them anyway. I flick the tassel of his hat. "Nothing you can do will hurt me."

"It's dou—"

"No. Any further outburst will be settled by having you

dismissed. Don't think I can't get someone else to do your job. It's easy enough and you're not even excelling at it."

His lips thin. "Very well. If that is all, My Lady."

"That is all."

He gives a bow and hurries from the room. Why do I feel like the best option just then would have been to stab him?

CHAPTER 29

Nash enters my sitting room without knocking and slams the door behind him. "I heard you threatened Ranen."

"Threatened? More like told him he needs to be doing his job."

He pinches the bridge of his nose. "Why do you have to make things so hard?"

"I'm not making anything hard. It's everyone else that appears to have a problem with me."

"You certainly are meant to be queen."

"What is that supposed to mean?" I demand.

He sighs. "Nothing."

"No. Really. Tell me what you mean. Inquiring minds are dying to know."

"Fine. You want to know? I'll tell you. You seem to believe the world revolves around you."

The words sting, but I don't let the hurt show. Instead, I find an excuse. "It does. I am the queen."

He shakes his head. "Exactly what I mean."

"And this is a problem?"

He sits on one of the chairs furthest from me. "No. I suppose not."

I want to scurry over to the chair next to his, to be closer, but I won't let myself show that sort of weakness. One shouldn't let themselves get attached to a person. Especially a person who could be gone any moment.

The thought of him being gone makes my stomach roil. I don't want him to leave me. I think back on our conversation. On anything other than him going away.

"What if I didn't want the world to revolve around me? How would things be different?"

He looks up at me, eyes wide. "Well, for starters, you would think of people besides yourself. You'd realize other people in this world have feelings and thoughts."

"Don't I listen to your thoughts?"

"Only because it gets you what you want."

"And what is it I want?"

He leans back into his chair. "You know, I'm not sure. I just know there's something."

"Well, that clears things right up."

"Hey. It's your life, not mine." He sits up straight again. "But truthfully you should be careful with Ranen. I know you're strong, but he's cunning."

"Are you saying I'm not cunning?"

"This what I'm talking about—you think everything revolves around you."

"But it does on this. You're speaking of Ranen having cunning plans concerning me."

"Which they do, but you're comparing your wits to his, instead of worrying about him."

"Ranen is harmless."

Nash scowls. "You need to worry about him more."

"Give me an example. What should I be worried about?"

He lowers his voice. "Did you know the last Queen was murdered?"

"I did." I force out the words.

His brows wrinkle together. "How? It's not common knowledge."

"I know more than you think." Though less than I should. Where is this conversation going?

He leans closer. "There's speculation that Ranen was the one behind it."

I laugh. I can't help it. That fool couldn't have anyone murdered. He's too weak to do anything.

He growls. "I wish you had a name, so I could curse it."

That sobers me up. "You have no right."

"And you have no right to take your life so casually. You are the queen of Valcora now. You have a responsibility to your people."

"You think I don't know that?"

"Occasionally you remember, but you often act like you don't."

I jump to my feet. "Do you want to have another wager over this?"

"I'm being serious."

"So am I."

"Fine. Let's wager. You win—I'll leave you alone about this. I win—you'll consider what I'm warning you about."

"Fine." I kick my shoes off.

To my surprise, Nash opens the door and says something to one of the guards. Instead of closing it like he usually does when he's finished, he leaves it open. He pulls out the low table and sets a chair on each side.

"What are you doing?" I ask. "Aren't we going to fight?"

"Oh we will, but not like you're thinking."

"What's that supposed to mean?"

The next moment, Eldim walks in the door, nako set in hand. The wooden box is closed, the intricately carved pieces inside. The outside holds pegs, where the pieces fit and move around.

"Oh, no." I shake my head. "That's not what we agreed on."

"You didn't specify the fight. This is what I pick. A game of strategy and cunning."

"That's not fair," I say.

Nash turns to Eldim. "Thank you. That will be all."

Eldim bows to me and then leaves the room and closes the door behind him.

"I'll even be a gentleman," Nash says. "I'll let you go first."

I grab the black pieces, though red is supposed to go first. Red is not a color I like. Nash lifts an eyebrow.

We set up our pieces strategically across our side of the board. I set mine in alternating rows, while he sets his up like an army. He is a guard. Maybe that makes a difference to what he chooses.

He jumps his first piece three pegs. "Your move."

We alternate moving pieces, until I lose my first one.

"Ugh." That's not a good sign.

The turns keep coming, and I snag a couple of his pieces. I grin, excited to have gotten one up on him.

Surprisingly, he grins back, like he hasn't a care in the world. "Ready to give in?" he asks.

"Never."

He captures one of my pieces then. And another. And another. Next thing I know, I only have one piece left, and unless he's stupid—which he clearly is not—he will get it next turn.

I move my piece closer to his in defiance. With a small smile, he captures it.

I lost. Of course I lost.

"Now will you take me seriously about Ranen?" he asks.

I purse my lips. I don't want to concede and yet— "I suppose I have to."

A look of satisfaction overcomes him. "Good. I don't like fighting with you. I'm sorry for the problems we've had."

His words send a sizzle of pleasure through me. "I agree. I don't like fighting with you, either. We shouldn't do it anymore. But if I'm going to heed your advice about Ranen, I want you to do something for me."

His gaze becomes guarded. "What's that?"

"I want to go out among the people."

"It's not safe. People have tried to take your life in the palace. Can you imagine what would happen if they found out you were outside these walls?" He sighs. "We could bring a lot of guards, but it's still risky."

"No guards. I'll go in disguise." Because it feels like too long since I had fresh air. I'm as much a prisoner here as I ever was at Daros's.

"I don't like it. Something could go wrong."

"Between you and me, I'll be fine."

He moves to the window and stares outside. He must let me. If he doesn't, I'll sneak out myself. "Why do you want to go?" he asks.

"I want to see the people as they are." And being their queen I can look at things in a different way. Maybe I'll realize what I missed before, when I was in a stupor.

When Nash turns, I can't tell what he's thinking.

"We can do this," he says. "But I have to be with you at all times, and it has to be a good disguise."

I suppress a squeal of delight—don't know where it even came from. "Thank you. Can we go this afternoon?"

"May as well get it over with. If you go get a disguise, and I'll find a way out of the palace."

This had better go smoothly.

CHAPTER 30

A DISGUISE IS EASY. I convince Inkga to give me one of her day dresses and a small bit of fabric. She complies with only a faint look of confusion. She's doing well since the poison worked its way out of her system. It's like she wasn't sick in the first place. I won't have someone's tray be sent up in a way that could be confused with mine again, though.

Once dressed, I take the extra fabric and wrap it around my hair. Best of all, the material doesn't match the dress, making me look even more like a Poruah. The only thing to take care of now is my face. A bit of dust should do the trick, once we're out of the palace.

I pass from room to room, waiting for Nash. He hasn't changed his mind, has he? I'll be upset if he has. I was quick to change, so maybe that's all it is. Still, I wait and wait.

About mid-afternoon, I answer the door to find Nash in peasant garb—simple brown cloth trousers with a loose cotton shirt. There's string crisscrossing at the neck of the cream shirt. He has boots that come up to his knees, and a cloak, probably to hide weapons in.

"Where is Her Majes—" He raises his eyebrows. "I'm impressed with your disguise."

"Thank you."

He holds out a second brown cloak. "For you."

"Thank you." I move to grab it, but he stops me.

"Let me help you." He grabs the cloak with both hands and whisks it around my shoulders, then ties it together in the front. "There. I wish we could do something to hide your face, but that would be more suspicious than leaving it in plain view. At least you're not familiar to the people yet, as your portrait hasn't been painted. Those who saw you were mostly Kurah class. It's doubtful they'll be out on the streets where we're going."

"Good. Let's go."

With a nod, Nash and I leave the room. "Afet, Wilric, come with us," he says. "The rest of you, stay here and make certain no one enters the queen's chambers."

The two guards follow after me, with Nash in the lead. He takes us through the palace until we reach a dead end with a potted plant on the side of an open window. After looking around, he does something to the wall. I can't tell what, but a secret door opens.

"Well done," I say.

"There still may be some men in the passageway, but hopefully they don't recognize you."

We get in the passageway, and Nash quickly fills the guards in on what we're doing.

"I didn't know they were coming with us," I say.

"You need more than only my protection. They'll keep their distance but will be there in case we need help."

I want to argue, but the longer we talk, the less time we'll have for sightseeing. "Fine."

We follow Nash through the long, dark passageway, with only a few torches here and there to light the way. We twist and turn through a serpentine path. It feels never ending, like the rest of the palace. Who designed this place, anyway?

I'm thinking about what we're going to find. What the people will be like. I haven't tried to care about them. They've always been obstacles in killing a target. I want to know what they're really like. I have to learn to care for them if I am their queen. No one ever cared for me, and I almost chose to end my life because of everything that happened to me. I don't want the same to happen to my people if there's something I can do to help.

When we come to another dead end, Nash pushes a stone on the wall, and it opens up behind a large bush outside the palace but still inside the walls.

There's barely room for us to go out. The branches claw at my arms, but my cloak protects me. We end up on a sunny strip of grass.

Nash strides toward the front entrance of the gate. Getting past the guards has my pulse racing. I take slow, steady breaths to try and calm it. What's the worst they can do? Realize I'm the queen? Then I can order them to let us out.

That does the trick. My heartbeat slows back to normal.

The entrance is wide enough for a wagon to come through. The portcullis is up, but guards line the way. None I recognize, but I take in their faces, trying to remember them.

"What are you doing out here, Nash?" the closest guard asks. "I haven't seen you since the queen made you Head Advisor."

"Thought it'd be a good day to go to the market. Stretch my legs," Nash replies.

"And who is this girl you have with you? She doesn't look familiar."

I give him what feels like a pretty smile.

"She's a new servant girl," Nash says. "Thought I'd take her with me and the boys."

"You know I can't let her back in without being vetted."

I keep my smile pasted on. I'm tempted to play the coquette, but without knowing him better, I don't know if it would help or hinder our cause. He has to let us out. I need to see my people.

"Come on, Piru. You know me. I work for the queen herself. I have her trust. You can let us out and back in when we return."

The guard shifts, eyeing the guards on either side of him.

"It's me," Nash says. "I'm always loyal to the queen."

Finally, the guard says, "If the girl's with you three, I'll trust her. Go on, then. Have a good time."

We pass by the guards without a problem, and then we're free. Out in the open.

Memories rush to me. That day I came here. How much despair I felt. How heavy my heart was with the grief of my actions. It's still here, simmering under the surface, though it's not as dark.

It doesn't take long for us to reach the market. Afet and Wilric take separate directions away from us. We see everything from a very few high-nosed Kurah class to Poruah afflicted with almaca, left out on the streets. I wish there was something I could do for them, but nothing can be done once someone has caught the fateful disease. The more spots they accumulate, the faster they wither away to nothing.

Now that I'm paying attention to the people instead of myself, it's strange. There are lots of downcast gazes and very little smiling or laughing even among those without almaca.

"What's wrong with everyone?" I ask Nash.

"Lots of things. Taxes. Lack of food. The uncertainty that comes with a new ruler."

"Aren't they used to it by now?"

He looks at me. Really looks. "Don't you know?"

I shake my head.

"Where did you come from?" His eyebrows are drawn together.

I face away from him. This would be a good time to tell him everything. He has a right to know what kind of monster I am. And yet, the words won't come. How do you tell someone you're an assassin? That you are capable of much depravity?

You don't.

"I'm unfamiliar with the people," I say, turning back toward him.

He presses his lips together, like he's trying to stop himself from asking more.

We wander through the stalls. I wish I'd brought some gold with me. Not that I need anything, but I could support the shop owners through buying something. Give money to the hungriest-looking children.

There's food out on the stalls, but not as much as I remember. Perhaps it's because I now have an abundance of food. I'm not starving.

Only a few purchase the food. The rest look at it longingly. "Why aren't more people buying things?" I ask.

"Because of the heavy taxes. They don't have enough." His voice holds a taint of bitterness.

"You disagree with how things are done?"

"Let's just say it's not my place to judge."

That's not helpful. "But as your queen, I'm asking for a direct answer."

"Shh. You don't want to give yourself away." He moves closer, like he expects someone to dart out with a sword at any moment.

I would push him away, except his presence is soothing. "No one has noticed. Answer the question."

"Fine. You want to know? I'll tell you. I think the taxes were a horrible idea. It's left very few Medi class. The poor are suffering, and even the rich are feeling its sting."

I look ahead, at a little girl staring at a table of apples with big, hungry eyes. "I wish I had some money to buy her one."

Nash doesn't hesitate. He strides over to the stall, purchases several apples, and hands them to the girl.

"Thank you, Mister," she says, looking at him like he's just saved her life.

Maybe he has.

She scampers off. Nash says, "I should have fed her sooner. Wish I could feed more of them. I'm distracted with trying to protect you."

"And you don't have enough money to feed them all."

"True, but I like to do what I can."

Am I doing all I can? "There are changes that need to be made."

"Major ones, that will take a lot of work to make happen." He continues walking, and I follow beside him.

"I don't know how to go about it." It's more work than I've had to do before. Ending a life is easy; making a living for a country is hard.

"I'm certain you'll figure out what's best."

"That's all you're going to give me?" I ask. "You're my Head Advisor. Shouldn't you offer more?"

"What more do you want me to add?" he replies.

"Something. Anything."

He opens his mouth, and then closes it again.

"What were you going to say?" I ask.

He shakes his head. "It isn't something we need to speak of."

"Now you've got me even more curious."

"My advice"—he sounds like he's getting back to the original subject, instead of answering my question—"is that you decide what changes you want to make, and go from there. It might take a law change, convincing people of something, or standing your ground when no one else agrees with you. Whatever it is, you have to set your mind to do it and follow through."

"Are you certain you haven't been Head Advisor before?" I ask.

He lifts an eyebrow.

"You know what you're talking about is all." But do I know what to do about it? I'm not sure. Maybe I should start with asking the first queen questions about queens of the past. Experiences they've had. Rules they've made, and the consequences of those laws.

"If you're willing," Nash says to me, "I think we should return."

"Yes, I've seen enough."

More than ever before.

CHAPTER 31

THE FIRST QUEEN *stands before me, clear as can be. "So, you found me."*

"I wanted to make certain you're real."

"That's smart. Good initiative, like a queen needs."

At least I did one thing right.

"You did more than one thing right. You've done a lot of things right. You're making a lot of progress, a good portion of which is due to Nash."

"You know Nash?"

"I do. He's good for you. You should open up to him more, instead of arguing with him."

"Because that would mean opening up with you too."

"It's true. It would help me as well. That doesn't mean it wouldn't be good for you. If you're not ready to talk to him, are you ready to talk to me?"

"No." Never. I can't open myself up to secrets that would hurt.

"You have to give in sometime. It's not good to keep things locked up inside."

I ignore her comment and say, "I need your help."

"That's why I'm here."

"How have the other queens ruled? How have they handled changing laws and doing what's best for the people?"

She gives me a look that I don't understand, which is strange; I can usually read people. Maybe it's because I'm in a dream. She says, "Queens don't always do what's best for the people."

"That much is evident. How can I?"

"You need to look into your heart. Your feelings. Deep down, you know what you should do."

It doesn't feel that way.

"Why is it so hard to find information on you?" I ask.

"Because I existed so long ago. Most knowledge about me was long ago lost or destroyed."

"Why destroyed?"

"Because people don't always appreciate what they have. Which is why I imbued myself into the Mortum Tura with magic. I knew things would be misplaced over time, but I wouldn't go missing, as long as they used the chalice to choose a new queen."

"How did you make the chalice?"

She sits down like she's on a chair, but really, she just floats in the middle of the blurry, colored space. "That is a story for another time. For now, we need to learn about your worth."

"I'd rather learn about the chalice."

"Of course you would, which is part of the reason it's so important to discuss your value. You're over an entire kingdom now. You can't be taking risks like climbing up the side of the building. What if you fell?"

"I never fall."

"But what if you did?"

I jolt awake. What was that sound?

There it is again—a faint patter of steps.

I slowly reach under my pillow and grab my dagger. Whoever it is, they aren't going to take my life. The first queen has a point. I'm over a whole country now. Besides, I won't be killed in my bed.

The whistle of something moving quickly though the air is the only warning I get that a knife is hurtled toward me. I dodge out of the way and then spring up on my feet. I take a step toward the window, where my attacker is, and kick him square in the chest.

He falls with a grunt. There's not time to light a candle and see who it is. I crouch down, dagger in hand, ready to attack.

There's a shuffle of movement from my attacker, but he's

moving away from me, not closer. My attacker is scared. I run toward the noise. A shadow moves. I jump on it, putting my dagger to its neck.

The person tries to shove me off, but I cling to them. "Move, and I'll jam this dagger through your neck," I say.

My attacker freezes in place.

"Guards," I call out as loud as I can. I don't need them, but it'd make things easier. Especially since my attacker is big. I'm glad I already I had my dagger to his throat before I realized how big he is. Not that it would have stopped me, but maybe I wouldn't have been so quick to jump on him, and the fight would have lasted longer. It would have been nice to spar with someone like I'm used to.

My door opens, and my two guards come in, one holding up a candle.

"Crimany," one of them says.

The other jumps to action, pulling out his sword and putting the blade between me and the big man. I pry myself from the attacker, who has a mean grin.

"Are you all right, My Queen?" Afet asks.

Before I can answer, the attacker swings around and knocks to the ground the soldier who drew out his sword. I throw my dagger at the burly man, and the blade sinks a couple inches into his back.

He howls and barrels at me. I jump back as his sword swings my way. Afet has no such problems. He knocks the attacker's sword with his own. Soon, the sound of metal against metal fills the room.

The first guard gets to his feet and glances at me.

"Go for help," I tell him.

Not that we have much use for it. By the time assistance arrives, this fight will be long over. The guard listens, though, and runs from the room. That or he's a coward.

The attacker doesn't seem to care about the guard going for help. He keeps at Afet, trying to get to me. I circle around with Afet as he moves to avoid being hit.

An opening appears. I pull back my arm, ready to throw, but at the last second I stop myself. It's that or have the blade embedded in the huge man's heart. I want to let it go, but I promised myself I wouldn't kill again. Even if it's to defend my own life, I can't bring myself to break that promise.

The moment is gone.

"Get out of my way," the attacker yells at Afet.

"On my honor, I won't leave the queen."

"She's no royal." The man growls and hurls himself into the fight.

I dive down and watch the men's feet move like a dance. As soon as Afet lunges to the side, I spring up and jam my dagger into the man's thigh.

He howls and flashes his blade my way. I dive back, but before I get there, Afet's sword blocks my attacker's.

The huge man continues to fight, even with my blade jammed in his leg. He leans heavily on his good one, his swordsmanship more than making up for his injury. I pull myself toward the bed and grab two more daggers from under my pillow.

Afet cries out. He's been hurt, a line of blood welling up across his arm. If I didn't know he was on my side before, now would tell me he is at least trying to appear that way. Not that I can ever be sure. I let my daggers go, one right after another, to sink into the attacker's upper left shoulder and his sword hand.

He drops his sword with a grunt. Even as it clangs to the floor, I'm grabbing another blade and running toward him. His good hand also has a dagger in it, but that doesn't stop me. I move right up to him, block his dagger with one hand, and press a blade to his neck with the other.

"Don't move." Venom oozes through my words.

"Are you well, Your Majesty?" Afet asks.

"Fine." Though I wouldn't be if I hadn't woken up.

The attacker isn't only big but has a scowl on his meaty lips. It's not enough to scare me. Is he sent from the same person as the others, or are there up to three people who want to take my life?

Knowing I'm not going to get an answer, I ask, "Who sent you?"

"Someone who wants you dead."

Afet shoves him to his knees, his arm still bleeding. "Your queen asked you a question."

The man has the audacity to laugh.

Thoughts of the torture I've been through hum to life. I'm confident I could get answers out of him, but at what cost? Could I forgive myself for becoming like Daros?

Guards run into the room, but I only pay them enough attention to make certain they're not a threat.

"You're going to spend a long time in the dungeon, unless you tell me who sent you," I say to my attacker. I'm confident he won't care, but I have to try.

"There's nothing you can do to me that'd make me admit anything," my attacker says.

Which makes me think of Daros sending him again. But he can't be the only cruel person out there. It could be anyone. "Take him away."

"I'll get him to the dungeon," Afet says. "We'll find out what we can from him."

"Thank you, gentleman. That will be all."

The guards leave the room with little fuss from my attacker, but Afet stays behind.

"Are you all right?" I ask him.

"It's a scratch."

A guard goes to the window. "There doesn't seem to be anyone else out there."

I nod. That doesn't mean I'm safe, though. I've got to find out who's sending these men after me.

CHAPTER 32

ONCE I'M by myself again, Nash rushes in the room. "Did he hurt you?"

He checks me over, moving his hands fervently over me. It's a pleasant sensation, until he stops.

Stepping back, he says, "Sorry. I got carried away. I don't know what I would do if he hurt you."

"I'm fine. I woke before he attacked."

"If you didn't..."

"But I did."

His caring for me is more than I expected. I thought he enjoyed my company, but not to this extent. It makes my heart warm.

He goes to the window and checks outside, like the guard did moments earlier. "I'll have guards I trust stationed outside your window at all times."

"That's not necessary."

He takes a step closer. "I assure you, it is. We would be lost without you. I'd be lost without you. I promise to do everything in my power to make certain you have a long reign."

Why is it that it's easier to believe him than it is to believe myself? "Why do you say 'we would be lost without you?' I haven't done much yet."

"But you will. I can tell you're going to save the people from their current circumstances."

How does he know that? I don't even know that.

"I'm going to spend the rest of the night outside your room," he says.

"You don't have to do that. You should get some rest."

"I do. I'll be fine."

Despite the heat blossoming through me, I say, "You're going to be falling asleep at our meetings tomorrow."

"If that's what it takes to keep you safe, I'll do it."

"I can keep myself safe."

He gives a half-smile. "Be that as it may, extra caution never hurt anything. I'm going to make certain you don't have to protect yourself any more than you have to."

This brings something to mind. "Have there been other attacks I'm not aware of?"

He drops his gaze. "I'm afraid there have been a few more. I've interrogated the men myself, but no one is talking. Now," Nash says, "try to get some sleep. I'll be around, so yell if you need anything. Anything at all."

"I will." Possibly.

He goes to the door and gives me another glance. "You're sure you're all right?"

"I'm perfectly well." Except for the shaking in my knees. No matter how many times my life is threatened, I'm always reminded of Daros.

Nash's gaze travels the length of me. Can he see my trembling? With a nod, he leaves and closes the door.

I hurt.

Why? I don't know. It's deep inside and makes me wish he didn't have to leave.

After checking the room and seeing there are guards outside my window, I move toward my bed. I'd like to climb up to the roof, but there's going to be none of that tonight. What time is it? It feels very late.

I plop onto my bed. It's surprising how quickly I got used to its softness. After a night like tonight, though, I can't bring myself to sleep on it. Instead, I drop down to the floor, on the side farthest from the window. I pull a pillow off the bed and settle it under my head.

The night is dark. Listless. I close my eyes.

The next thing I know, light is streaming in above the bed. Morning's here. How did I not toss and turn more? How wasn't I riddled with fears? No nightmares. No lady in green. Nothing but soothing sleep.

I roll over. Nash sits with his back against the wall.

I brush the sleepiness from my eyes. "What are you doing?"

"I was so worried about you, I couldn't stay away. I had to make certain you were safe."

Peace hums through me. "I have guards watching over me. Not to mention my own skills."

"I know. It should be enough, but the thought that something might happen to you kept haunting me. I couldn't take that chance."

Dark circles hang under his eyes. His gaze, though, is peaceful. More than that—something is in it. Something I can't read. "You should have gotten some sleep, but…" Can I tell him? I must. "I'm grateful for your caring."

"It's the least I can do."

"Why do you say that?"

"Because it's true. You're worth taking care of."

I flush. Nothing like this has ever been said about me before. My only value has been my proficiency at killing. That doesn't matter to him. Somehow, he genuinely cares for me.

"Nash, I—"

"Breakfast," Inkga says coming in through the door. "What are you doing on the floor?"

I give her a sheepish smile. "It's more comfortable."

"Hmpf." She brings the tray over to me. I sit up, and she sets it on my lap. "Nash thought you might like this brought in here this morning, after the commotion of last night. It's been checked over by the new court poison checker"

"That was... thoughtful." I am in awe of Nash.

Utter awe.

It's the most anyone has ever done for me—thinking of my needs. I don't know how to respond.

"Do you need a tray, Nash?" Inkga asks, interrupting my thoughts.

"No. I should get going." He stands. "I have some guards I need to speak to this morning, and a prisoner who needs attention."

I make to move the tray. "I'm coming with."

"It's all right, Your Majesty," he says. "I've got everything under control, and I will report back to you when I'm finished."

He bows his head toward me, nods at Inkga, and is out of the room. I stare at the closed door.

"He is rather handsome, isn't he?" Inkga says. "I know the queen can't have relations, but he's mighty fine to look at."

Jem said as much about relations earlier, but I didn't pay attention. Now I wish it were otherwise.

CHAPTER 33

"Jem is set to speak with you this morning," Inkga tells me as she pins my short locks off my face.

Another night with no dreams or first queen. I don't mind, though. "I need to find out what's going on with the prisoners." I can't wait for Nash's word. The thought of them down there, knowing who sent them, eats at me.

"And you will. After you speak with Jem."

"Very well, then." But I can't help but think of the prisoners, even as she finishes helping me get ready and I go to the sitting room.

Moments later, there's a knock on my door. Inkga answers it for me, presents Jem, and then leaves us.

Jem curtsies and picks the chair one over from mine. Perhaps we need a buffer between us, to prevent any major confrontations.

"What have you come to speak about?" I ask.

"Your Majesty, first, I wanted to say I'm sorry."

Not what I expected. "For what?"

"I heard you were attacked again last night."

I wave her off. "It was only a trifle." I'm more concerned with who's behind it.

She opens her mouth. Closes it. Says, "Yes, Your Majesty. Still, we're all glad you're safe."

I'm in the mood for blunt honesty. "Are you?"

She shrinks back into her chair. "I am. I promise you that."

I don't know. I get the feeling she's hiding something. "Is that all you wanted to say?"

"No. I wanted to help teach you about court manners. Maybe speak to you about the ball."

I stand. "I'm not in the mindset for manners today. As to the ball—talk to Nash's sisters and Monkia about that."

"But, Your Majesty, this will reflect on you. We need time to teach you before you're presented and coronated."

"Some other time. If you'll excuse me." I stand, not caring if she will or not.

I head to the door and open it. A grimace passes by so quick I almost miss it.

"It's been a pleasure, Your Majesty," she says with a curtsy.

"I'm sure you have much more pleasant things in your life." I will never be one of them.

"As you say." With those brave words, she takes off.

Maybe she has more of a spine than I thought, even if she'd rather have the throne. Or something. I can't pinpoint what she's hiding.

In any case, I want answers from the prisoners. I head out the door, where Wilric, Afet, and a few other guards accompany me.

I studied the maps enough to know where the dungeons are. It takes some time to get there, with my guards trailing behind me.

When we get to the entrance, Wilric stops me. "Are you certain you want to go down there, Your Majesty? There are many criminals down there who would like to see your downfall."

Many, huh? "I've been in worse places."

I march forward. The stairs are steep but well lit. The place smells of dampness and body odor. As I climb down the stairs, I think of what awaits. What I don't expect to find is a desk. The man sitting at it is speaking with Nash.

The little room is dank, but well lit, with nothing in it besides the large desk. It has a hallway leading off to where I assume the prisoners are kept. It's nothing like I expected a dungeon to be, but perhaps that's because this is only the entrance.

Nash looks up at me, eyes sparkling until he grows somber. "To what do we owe the honor of your presence, Your Majesty?"

Just being around him makes my insides feel warm and gushy. It's not a feeling I can afford, here in the dungeon. "I want to know what progress is being made with the would-be assassins."

Nash's expression doesn't change, but the guard at the desk cringes.

"We've acquired no further information from them," Nash says.

What I was afraid of. "Would you take me to those who have threatened my life?"

"Yes, Your Majesty." He turns and after making sure I'm following, heads deeper into the dungeon.

We pass a good dozen empty cells. They are made of bars and have six beds apiece. The beds are bunked together in twos. Other than those and a chamber pot in the corner, the rooms are empty. If they can be called *rooms*.

We get to the first occupied cell, and I don't recognize any of the faces there. A few turn and give me heed, but none say anything. Several more rooms have people in them, all unfamiliar to me.

"Who are these people?" I ask.

"They have committed lesser crimes, Your Majesty. Such as stealing," Nash responds. When we come to a cell that has only one person, he stops. "This is the place where your attackers start. We keep them sectioned off from everyone else."

"Wise."

"They haven't given us anything useful. We're trying our best to get answers from them while still remaining humane."

What would happen if we weren't humane? It doesn't matter. I won't stoop lower than I previously have. Not that it matters. I'm already blackened.

"Let's question one of them. Pick at random." My fingers itch to grab a dagger. It wouldn't be the first time I used it to get information out of someone, but I can do better than that. I have to.

"You." Nash points at the prisoner in the middle cell. "Answer the questions the queen has for you."

I expect the man to ignore us, but he jumps up and bangs his hands against the bars. He's a big man—burlier than any of the guards I've seen. Bigger even than the man who attacked me last night His facial hair has grown out to be a little longer than scruff. He glares at me with his dark eyes something fierce. "You are not my queen."

Beside me, Nash tenses.

I cross my arms. "Who is, then?"

His nose flares.

"Come on now," I say. "If you're so set on having a different ruler, who is it?"

"Like I'd tell you."

"Is it someone outside the palace?" I watch carefully for signs of recognition.

He scowls but gives away nothing further.

"Is it someone inside the palace?"

He shifts his gaze the tiniest fraction.

"In the palace, then. Someone on the council?"

He laughs, and I have to wonder if I'm off base. If he was sent by Daros, he'd be so well trained that he could give me clues he believed I wanted. It makes me want to punch him in the face. Of course, if he was trained by Daros, that'd be unlikely to give me answers anyway. Even if he wasn't, a good assassin doesn't reveal anything.

I'm wasting my time.

I curl my lips at him in disgust. "Things would go easier if you told us what you know."

"You have no idea what you're dealing with."

I want to roll my eyes but refrain. "The same could be said of you."

"Would you like to speak to another prisoner?" Nash asks when I step away from the cell.

"I doubt it would do much good. Not without"—torture, and even then it's questionable—"better techniques."

We pass the three cells, and I expect that to be all, but then we come to another occupied one. "Who is this?"

A muscle in Nash's jaw flexes. "Another who tried to get to you and didn't make it. His intentions were made clear by the other things he's said since capture and the way he was hiding around the palace. The others are in similar circumstances."

"Others? How many?"

"Besides the three you interacted with, eight."

Eleven people have tried to kill me? I've only been Queen for a few weeks. "And no clue who sent them?"

"Forgive me, Your Highness. We haven't been able to glean anything from any of them."

"Is it normal to have so many attacks?" I ask.

"You've had a couple more than average, but that doesn't mean much. They could be after you for any variety of reasons."

Wonderful. I'm a target for so many besides just Daros.

He shows me the rest of the cells. None of the men pay me any mind or act like we're there at all. I could question them. Doubt I'd learn anything without resorting to methods I refuse to use.

"Very well, then," I say. "Thank you for showing me around. Let me know if any progress is ever made with them."

"Of course," Nash says. "I'll see you out."

He walks me through the corridor, past the guard at the desk, and up the stairs. Once we're back in the palace hallway, where sunlight is streaming in through the window, everything should be brighter. But it's not. It's a bleak outlook.

"Sooner or later, one of them will kill me," I tell him, ignoring the guards around us.

His gaze becomes fierce. "I won't let them."

"It's inevitable. Unless we find out who's sending them all, my life is mine for only so long." I turn and walk away, ignoring the pressure on my chest.

CHAPTER 34

THE FIRST QUEEN *is sitting on air when I see her several feet from me. Her green dress is draped around her, as the colors of the sunset fill the air.*

"Your life is in danger," she says.

"That much is clear." Though it's thrilling to have people attack me.

"Your conclusions are dangerous. I thought we moved past this point."

I feel her prodding. Looking for something in my mind. I close it down, not wanting her to intrude. "It's fine. I'm well trained."

"It's easy to tell that's the case."

"What would you have of me?" I ask.

"Have you made any decisions regarding the changes you want to make?"

I sigh. I wish there was a place to sit.

"You can sit. Think of a chair being underneath you, and it will be."

I do as she says. Surprisingly, it works, though there is nothing but swirls of color under my feet. "Where are we? Is this a dream?"

"No. This is something more than a dream. A place in between dreams, life, and death."

"That doesn't make any sense."

"It does, with magic."

"Do I have magic? Is there a way to learn it?" I ask.

She regards me solemnly. "You have much power."

"And can I learn to harness it? Can I cast spells and make things like the Mortum Tura?"

"Did you decide what to do about the laws? What direction you're going to go in, as queen?"

Why doesn't she answer my questions?

"Why don't you answer mine?"

"Very well," I say. "I've not decided what direction I want to go in. I want to help the people. To be a good queen. But I don't know how to do it. I don't want to make a mistake."

She stands and walks toward me, but stops before she gets to me. "It's all right to make mistakes."

No, it isn't.

She reaches out, like she wants to touch my shoulder, but I flinch away.

With a sigh, she sits back down. "I promise you're safe here. You can make mistakes. Everyone does—even a queen."

"Was that what happened with the last queen? Deedra? Did she make a mistake in raising taxes?"

"Is that what you think?"

"I'm asking what you think."

"I'm here to guide you. But yes, Deedra did raise taxes."

"Was it a mistake, though? Did you council her for or against it?"

"Let's just say Deedra listened to me less and less, during her reign."

"Why?" I want to know. Want to understand.

The first queen looks somewhere over my shoulder. "It's hard to explain, but I'll try. Deedra was a very headstrong girl. Despite wanting to end her life, she quickly changed. She knew what she wanted, and that was power. It's something the Mortum Tura can't overcome. I tried to stop her—to guide her to a better way of life—but it couldn't be helped. Sometimes queens are like that, despite my precautions. Usually I can find a woman who is after what's best for the people, and not for herself, but it doesn't always happen. Like in Deedra's case."

How sad that must be—to make a way for your country to not be *ruled by power-hungry people, only to have one come about anyway.*

"Did you try to connect with her like you do with me?"

"I tried, but I fear I failed."

"Even queens make mistakes."

She smiles at me, soft and genuine. "Exactly."

CHAPTER 35

NASH and I go over things for the ball all morning. It's mentally exhausting work, but I'm glad to be getting it done. Only a few days left until it's here.

"Do you know how to dance?" Nash asks.

"Well enough to get by." I am ready to take on any situation.

"For a queen, you have to do better." He stands in the middle of my sitting room, the furniture still pushed aside. "If you would please come here, you can show me what you know."

I don't move. "Without music?"

"The steps are the same whether we have music or not. Unless you would prefer to go to the ballroom?"

Too many eyes there. "Fine."

I get to my feet and move over to him. He bows. I start to curtsy, but he stops me. "If you were anyone else, you would curtsy, but a queen never lowers herself to anyone."

Something about that feels wrong, but I press the thought away.

I take his left hand in my right. His palm is warm against mine, hardened with calluses. It's a hand fit for a soldier. Good thing being my Head Advisor hasn't softened him.

He pulls away. "The queen isn't supposed to touch anyone. I've been negligent in that area. I apologize."

I grimace. It was so nice feeling the contact. I wish he didn't remember that rule. Wish he didn't want to say he's sorry.

He puts his hand up, and I raise mine but we keep them a good inch apart. As we circle, the warmth of his skin travels through me, to my arm and up my shoulder, to spread throughout my body. Even without touching, there's something fantastic about being so close. It's unlike anything I've ever felt. As we move our hands away from each other, the feeling leaves. When we switch hands and bring them close together, the feeling returns, stronger than before.

What is this? I can't look him in the eye, though I should.

We move apart, and I face him now. I walk back a step as he stays still. Moving closer to him, I feel his heat.

He steps back as I stay still. Immediately, I miss the closeness. What is getting into me? We continue the dance, moving back and forth, in circles, and around the room. I barely think of what I'm doing, focusing instead on his hands near mine.

"You dance beautifully." His voice is barely above a whisper.

Heat rises inside me at the compliment, but there's nothing I can do to stop it. "You dance well yourself. How did a guard come to learn this?"

"My mother."

"Ah."

We finish the dance, and he bows. I wish we could continue practicing. I should have stumbled. Made some sort of false move. Then we could have continued on for some time. Rather, we take a seat.

"Now," he says. "About music—what would you like?"

I haven't a clue. "What do your sisters have to say about it?"

"They think getting several different music groups and rotating them throughout the night would be good."

"It would. We could highlight both the Poruah, Medi, and Kurah classes."

"Right. It would go right along with our theme. I'm sure we can find groups to play for us if this is what you want."

"I do. Have at least three different groups."

"Consider it done. I'll have my sisters and the ladies in waiting help pick them out. Between them, we should have some good variety."

A thought strikes me. "Have we sent out the invitations?"

"We have, in fact. It was one of the first things we did. Not only that, but we sent out proclamations throughout all of Valcora announcing the coronation ball."

"If there are no people there, then it won't be because they didn't know about it."

"There will be people there," he says. "I think it's time for a break. I have something to show you." He stands. "Come on."

I resist the urge to take his hand again. "Where are we going?"

"It's a surprise." He gives a sly grin.

Once we're out in the hall, he tells the guards to follow us. We make our way through the hallways, as I try to mentally picture where we are going. I know the bottom floor quite well by now, but I don't go on the other floors as much. We head up three flights of stairs.

All this walking up stairs is reminding me of being at Daros's. The stairs were my soothing journey to being alone.

Unless Daros tried to interrupt my solitude that is.

Shoving the negative thought away, I focus on the rest that's taking over my soul. The peace that fills this area. A solemn thing that leaves me wanting to whisper. That could just be remnants of Daros's house as well, but I'd like to think it's more.

We reach another hall, and Nash says something to the guards. Three of them plant themselves at our end of the corridor while the other two make their way to the far side.

The hall is huge in both length and height. What really draws my attention are the pictures on either side. Instead of the usual Valcora landscapes, there are portraits of women.

"Who are they?" I ask in a hushed tone, though I can guess.

"They are past rulers. This is the Hall of Queens." Nash's

response is subdued as well, as if we both recognize the importance of this place.

I look around in wonder, taking in women of all sorts of beauty and different ages. The youngest looks about as old as me. They're all finely dressed, but that's the only thing they have in common. I take them in one by one, reading the names off the bottom of the frame as we go.

None of them looks like the woman from my dreams.

When we're about three quarters of the way down the hall, the images end and naked stone walls greet us.

"This is where your portrait will hang, once it's painted," Nash says.

I'm not sure I'm ready to sit for one. Not brave enough yet, even if Daros already found me. "Are these all of the queens?" I ask.

"As far as I'm aware, yes. They are."

I go back over each portrait, searching. He patiently follows after me, giving me space yet comfort with his presence. I still look around my surroundings often and keep an ear out for trouble, but otherwise I'm focused on the task.

When we're back to where we started, I say, "This can't be all of them."

"Why not?" He looks puzzled.

Now is the perfect opportunity to tell him about my dreams. About the first queen. "Jem said not all queens got painted before they died."

"They—uh—got their portrait after they passed away."

"That's awkward."

"Yeah. But they are remembered, even if they didn't serve long."

"What's the shortest anyone's reigned?" I ask.

He grimaces. "Two days."

I almost beat that. "What's the longest anyone's reigned?"

"Seventeen years."

That's not bad. But I'm getting off topic. "Are you certain there's no one missing?"

"There could be, but I was told they're all here. Why do you ask?"

"Just curious."

He studies me, and I focus back on the nearest portrait.

Where is the first queen? Why isn't she among these pictures?

CHAPTER 36

I'M GETTING ready for bed when a thought crosses my mind.

"What do you like to do in your free time?" I ask Inkga.

"I don't know. There isn't much of it. I suppose I like to spend time with family and friends."

I don't like talking about families. The closest thing I had to one was Daros. He found me abandoned. Alone and ready for his tutelage. Forcing the thoughts away, I ask, "What's it like to have a friend?"

"You haven't had one before?"

"I don't think so."

"Maybe you did, at some point?"

I sigh. "It's not something I like to dwell on, but…"

"Go on. I promise it's safe with me." Her voice is comforting.

It may be; it may not be. Either way, I find myself relating the tale. "I didn't have a lot of people around in my childhood. One day, I met a woman while I was outside." Training, running, and jumping over obstacles. Even as a kid I worked hard. But Inkga doesn't need the specifics. "This woman was kind to me. She talked to me like no one else did. She kept coming back whenever I was outside. When she discovered I didn't know how to read, she began teaching me."

"How old were you at the time?"

"I was about eight. She taught me what she could over a few months. One day she said life was too rough on me. I shouldn't have to work so hard as a child. She wanted to take me away from that. At least she said she did." My eyes burn—a sensation that's been coming too often since I moved into the palace. I stare at nothing, until the feeling goes away. "She promised to come get me the next day."

"What happened?"

I swallow. "I never saw her again." She abandoned me, just like everyone else.

"What did your parents think of it?"

"I have none."

Inkga is silent for some time. "You know, I used to think being the queen would be wonderful. I used to even think about trying for it myself."

"What stopped you?"

"Death. I'm not ready to die. And with so many failing, it wouldn't be worth it. That, and my friends and family again. If I died, I wouldn't be around them."

Our conversation is going everywhere, but there are so many things I want to know. "So why did you think it would be wonderful to be queen? You don't sound like you feel that way any longer."

"Not after seeing what you've been through. The threat of death hasn't stopped just because you became queen. I'd much rather do your hair and help you with your clothes."

"Can you tell me something?" I ask.

"Of course. What is it?"

"How do you know someone is a friend? That you can really trust them?"

"You don't know?"

"Like I said, I don't think I ever had one."

She gives me a pitying look that makes me want to crawl in a deep dark hole. "*Friend* definition then. They are kind of hard to describe. A friend is someone you can spend time with and enjoy their company. Well... most of the time. You can still get irritated with them sometimes." She gives a little laugh. "But a person whose company you enjoy. You relish doing things with them. It's someone you can talk to, who doesn't only listen, but also understands. They are happy when you feel joy and sad when you have pain. They warn you against foolish decisions but support you when you go through with them anyway. And then, when you fall, they're there to pick you up."

That sounds wonderful. "How do you make friends?"

"The truth is it's easier to make friends when you act softer."

"Am I harsh?" I demand.

"Like that."

"Like what?"

"Like you just were. You never ask anything. You boss people around. It's like you were born to be a queen, not a friend."

"I wasn't born to be anything." But an assassin.

"It's all right," she says. "We can try. You just need to work on your tone. How you say things can be more important than what you say. Your thoughts are good, they're just a little brass and unrefined."

I work hard to think about my words. "What you mean is that I need to change."

She glances at the floor. "If you don't mind, Your Majesty. If this is something you want—to have friends. To make people like you, it would be good to practice, yes."

"Would you help me practice?" It's almost anguishing to speak politely.

"You said that very well. It would be my honor to help you."

"How do we start? And please, take a seat. It's strange, having you stand while I'm sitting."

"If you're sure," she says.

"Positive."

She takes a seat, instantly making me feel better, though she sits at the very edge of her chair.

"Begin," I say.

"Right." She clears her throat. "Let's say you're eating dinner, and it's something you hate. How would you react in public?"

"I eat everything." Starving will do that to you.

"All right. What if someone brought you a gift you didn't like? What should you do?"

I think. Hard. "Depends on the gift." Most of what I've received has been things like daggers and poisons.

"It was something you didn't like," Inkga prods.

"I'd probably say I'm not interested in it."

"There's a perfect instance we can work on. Whether you like it or not, you need to accept it graciously, saying *thank you*. Even better if you can find some way to compliment the gift."

"Even if I hate it?" This is harder than I thought.

"Even then. They've taken the time to get you something and bring it to you. Many times they'll be extravagant gifts that you'll enjoy. Other times, they might be from someone who has little possessions and brought you all they have. It might not look like much, but to them, it's everything. You need to keep this in mind when you respond."

"I can understand that better." Besides what I needed for my work, I had little.

"So what would you say to someone who gives you a gift you don't like?"

"I'd say *thank you*. Maybe say it's beautiful or useful or thoughtful."

"Excellent. Now, make sure you calm your tone."

I reach inside myself, pulling out the calmest tone I can think of. "Like this?"

She hesitates. "Um… that was a nice try, but think of something soft. Something soothing. Try to emulate that."

Emulating is what I do; it shouldn't be hard. I think of a soft breeze kissing my skin. "Thank you for helping me."

"That was perfectly done, Your Majesty." Inkga claps her hands, eyes gleaming, smile wide.

"I'm glad because I want the people to feel like they can approach me so I can help them."

"The effort to improve will make you the best queen ever."

The words stir me. Can I be a good queen? Am I capable of it? I don't know.

CHAPTER 37

IN THE HAZE, *I make out the first queen. She's dimmer than usual, the colors not as bright.*

"It's because you've got a lot on your mind," she says. Her voice sounds far away. "And you aren't in a deep sleep. We haven't much time tonight."

I get right to asking what I want to know. "Why aren't you among the pictures of all the queens?"

"I never had my likeness painted. Even if I did, it'd be destroyed or lost. They didn't take good care of my things."

"But you're in that history book."

"Yes. Perhaps a few more items have been passed down about me, but my image was not drawn in that book while I was alive. At least, not with my knowledge."

It doesn't make a difference, yet I wish there were more signs of her. Some way to connect me to her, other than through just dreams. I should be grateful I found her picture at all.

"I see preparations for the ball are coming along nicely," she says. "Are you ready for it? Ready to be coronated and become the queen in more than name?"

"I don't know. But I'm trying."

"That's all that matters. You need to do your best, and that's good enough."

"Is it truly?" Because it doesn't feel like it.

"You'll have to learn that for yourself, of course. What I say won't matter if you don't internalize it."

"I'll keep at it." Is this what a friend is like?

"I know you will."

CHAPTER 38

I've just finished getting ready for the day when Inkga says, "The ladies in waiting have requested an audience."

My initial thought is to turn them down, but I'm trying to be better. "I will see them. Is my sitting room big enough for all who wish to visit?"

"I believe it is, Your Majesty."

"Then I will see them there. Thank you, Inkga." I let her lead the way out of the room. As she goes to the door, I take a seat. Several minutes later, she admits my ladies in waiting.

"Please let me know if you need anything further," Inkga says.

I nod, and she hurries off. There are a good thirteen of them, all elaborately dressed like I was before Inkga helped me acquire better clothing. The result is a rather humorous array of wide skirts, lace, and fluff that has me holding in a laugh.

As one, the ladies in waiting move to the center of the room and dip into deep curtsies.

"You may rise and be seated," I say.

They take seats, barely having enough room for them all but they fit. Before I can say anything, they pull out one form of hand-work or another. They're settling in. *Lovely.*

"To what do I owe the pleasure of your company?" I ask.

"We wanted to spend time with our queen," Faya, the oldest lady in waiting, says. "We've been remiss in being with you. I hope we can remedy that now."

Nothing I want to say would be well received, so I stay silent.

"Would you like some embroidery to work on, Your Majesty?" Jem asks with a hint of mockery in her voice.

"I'm fine."

"But a queen must know how to do handwork."

"No. In fact, I want you all to put whatever you're working on away. It's vastly annoying. If you want to continue it on your own time, fine. But you will not use it as an excuse to avoid looking at me." I feel quite smug. I shouldn't have said anything, but it drives me mad.

The ladies hustle to put their things away—all except Jem.

"If Your Majesty will forgive me, this is something that's taken place for as long as anyone can remember." She doesn't sound sorry at all. "It's not a tradition we should break."

"Useless traditions will not remain under my rule." She better not say anything further, or I will need to find some consequence for it. From everything I've learned, no one is supposed to speak to a queen in such a manner. Disagree with me? All right, but do it respectfully.

She flutters her hands over her fabric and needle, as if she can't decide what to do with them. Finally, she puts them away somewhere inside her voluminous skirts.

It's a relief, until she says, "Perhaps, then, we should speak of your wardrobe."

"My new clothes suit me well." Beyond well. I love having pants to climb around in and not so many layers and fabric when I wear a dress. Most importantly, all of them have lots of places to hide daggers.

"But as queen, you should know that whatever style you choose will be picked up by the very elite. Borkus should have talked to you about designs worthy of your position." Jem's eyes flash at me.

"I'm afraid he is not in on the consultation of my clothing. My maid and I have come up with everything that's needed for my wardrobe. We will speak of it no more." She's crossing into so many topics I don't want to discuss. It's like she knows how to wheedle her way under my skin.

"How about use of dinnerware?" Jem asks, her tone almost gleeful. "We need to make certain you do not make a fool of yourself the first time you eat a meal in public."

"Jem, I would prefer if you removed yourself from the room." My words surprise me, but I'm grateful I said them. I'm used to being spoken down to, but it ends now. "If you wish to remain, you will stay silent."

Her face grows pale, but she says nothing more. Next to her, Inyi pouts, but Faya has a twinkle in her eyes. Perhaps Jem has needed to be set down for some time.

"What did you talk about with the last queen?" I ask.

"None of us were ladies in waiting for the last queen," a woman who looks to be in her thirties says. She has dark hair, dark eyes, and golden skin.

"What is your name?" I ask her.

"Lipla, Your Majesty."

"Very well, Lipla, what happened to the last ladies in waiting?" I ask.

"They were the first to take the Mortum Tura when the last Queen died."

I pinch my lips together. So much death. Can I never get away from it? "And you all will try for the throne when I am dead?"

No one answers.

"The answer must obviously be *yes* if no one is brave enough to say it."

Jem's face is contorted, like she's trying to hold an answer in. Perhaps if I didn't forbid her from speaking, she would be brave enough. It's not something I'll know at this rate, though.

"It is true, Your Majesty," Faya says. "We were all deemed finished with our training so we could try the Mortum Tura."

"And that is what you all want? To become queen?" I ask.

They stare at the floor. No telling if they would have passed the test. Likely not, if it was something they were trying for. None of them would have become queen then.

This begs a further question. "Are you trying to have me killed?"

The room becomes a clamor of *No, Your Majesty.*

I wait for them to simmer down. "It seems you protest too much. Still, I know you've been helping with the ball, and I'm grateful for your help. I hope you will decide I'm fitting as your queen and will stop trying to take my life." I look each of them in the eye as I speak. Faya and Jem are the only ones who meet my gaze.

Faya has a soft expression, which doesn't mean much. She could be hiding anything, but for some reason, my heart wants to trust her.

Jem is much different, looking at me with open defiance. I wouldn't be surprised to find she's the one behind the threats on my life. I just have to find a way to prove it.

CHAPTER 39

IT'S LATE AT NIGHT, and I'm hanging out on the roof. There are two moons out tonight—one tinted gray, the other blue. They shine down on the country. *My country.*

It doesn't seem like nearly enough, being out here all alone. I wish Inkga was with me. Or Nash. The two of them are good company, though I do get irritated with them on occasion.

They feel kind of like how Inkga described *friends.* Maybe, they could be my friends. What would they think of that? Would they turn me away? Am I only a job to them? I hope not, but I don't know how to be more.

It's growing chilly, the night air cool against my clothes. I'm grateful Inkga took me seriously about pants being something I want. They make traveling to the roof much easier. I sigh and stand to walk to the edge of the roof. I don't care if someone sees me tonight. The worst they can do is make me get back down. They won't be able to stop me from wandering.

As I roam, I hear talking, but I'm too far to understand what they're saying. I lean closer over the edge, but I still can't hear them. I'm about to let it go, but then a man raises his voice. Ranen.

I crawl my way down, like I would if I was going to my room, but instead, I hang on the wall right outside the window. The voices are loud enough for me to not only hear, but also identify here.

A voice says, "Why didn't you have Jem go before this stupid urchin?"

I knew I was right about Jem.

"She pushed her way forward," Ranen says. "How was I supposed to know she wouldn't die? Everyone else did."

"It doesn't matter now. We have to figure a way around this."

"There is no way around it," Ranen practically shouts. Does he not worry about being overheard? "Jem would have bent under my will, but this queen will have nothing to do with me. I've tried to please her—doing what she asked, to get back in her good graces—but it's done no good. Neither have any of the assassins I've sent after her."

I whisk in a breath. At least now I know who was behind some of them. How many did he send?

I peek around the edge. Ranen has his back to me. His partner is Borkus, the Head of Design. He's facing me, but doesn't seem to see me.

I slide in the window, move up behind Ranen, and put a knife to his throat before he knows I'm here. "You dare dishonor me?"

His partner's mouth falls open, and he takes a step back.

"Forgive me, Your Highness. I didn't—" Ranen starts.

"No excuses." My phrase, all too familiar—though from a master's lips—jolts me back to the circumstances.

I yank my knife away from Ranen and snick it back into its case in my boot. Too many eyes for me to finish the job, even if it's just my own and another man's. He isn't a job anyway.

Besides, I promised not to kill. If I keep my knife out, he won't survive.

I'm about to call out, when cool metal presses against my neck. Borkus's eyes are wide. Ranen is still in front of me. Who—?

"Your Majesty will forgive me for meeting under these circum-stances." Faya's voice is soft and grandmotherly as ever, despite the fact she's holding a blade against me.

"What are you doing?" I ask, hoping to distract her so I get the upper hand. She can't be nearly as well trained as I am, but she is the one with the leverage.

She laughs. "You are a fool who's easily misled. I knew you would suspect Ranen from the start. He makes no secret of those he dislikes."

Ranen hisses but doesn't deny her words.

"But why you, Faya? Why are you attacking me? You were always the kind one." My words come out clear and strong.

"Kind?" She laughs, and for the first time since I met her, she sounds mad. "My only kindness is that I'm about to put you out of your misery."

"You helped send killers after me?" I have to keep her talking. Keep her from pressing that blade any farther into me.

"Helped? No, nameless girl, Ranen and I were the ones that sent them."

I can't help my gasp. "But why?"

"Because I want control of the country."

"Except they just said Jem would have been the one, not you."

"Of course Jem. I wouldn't take the Mortum Tura and risk my life, but I had to be in a position close to the Queen. If Jem had beat you to the Mortum Tura, she would have been crowned, and together, Ranen, Borkus, and I could have controlled her."

"I think you're mistaken. Jem would never be controlled by anyone."

She jams the blade harder against my neck. "That's where you're wrong. She only appears strong to you to hide her own weaknesses. She relied heavily on Ranen and me. Always. Thought I was like her grandmother, who passed away years ago. I could have control of the entire country without assassins coming for my own life? But no. You had to come along and push your way forward. Had to make yourself queen. Well, no more."

"How did you get to the assassins?" I ask, slowly going for my pocket where I have another dagger sheathed.

"It's easy. The hard part was your unexpected handling of them. If anything, I thought the poison would do you in, but we had to catch on to that as well."

"You were the one behind the poor boy that killed himself?"

She cackles. "I took care of him. Made him write his own note and everything. You never even suspected the person who brought the trays to your rooms was the one who put the poison in your cups, but it was easy for me to do. And now, here we are, with your life in my hands."

"Do her in, Faya," Ranen says with a sneer. "We can't drag this out much longer. If her guard suspects she's gone missing, they'll start a search for her."

"Couldn't have played into our hands any better." Borkus folds his arms and smirks at me.

I wanted to know who put the attack out on my life. I've found all three of them.

Before Faya can react, I grab my dagger out of my pocket and jam it backwards into her stomach. She drops the blade from my throat with a hiss of pain. I pull out the dagger, ready to defend myself.

"*Guards,*" I call out, hoping they are somewhere nearby. We're not far from my room, but there could be trouble if they don't come. Not that I can't handle a bit of trouble. Still, I back all the way up toward my entrance. Best to be prepared.

Ranen turns on me. "Grab her," he hisses to Borkus. "Stab her in the heart."

"I'd like to see you try," I say as I kick back at Faya, pushing her farther from me.

Ranen comes barreling at me, clumsy and unrefined. I twist away at the last moment. Borkus grabs me from behind. I elbow him in the gut and push off him, using the momentum to punch Ranen in the chest.

Ranen grunts and falls to the ground.

"Wimp." I want to kick him while he's down, but I do have manners. Some.

Borkus tries to escape out the hall, but the guards come at that moment and grab him before he can go anywhere. I recognize Afet and Wilric, but none of the others.

"Partnering with Ranen was a mistake," I tell Borkus and Faya.

Faya pays me no mind. She's clutching her stomach and groaning, her fingers turning crimson where she's holding her wound.

"What happened?" Wilric asks, even as he moves toward my attackers.

"These are the three responsible for the attacks on my life."

He looks at Faya and then turns for me. "We have to call for a healer. Unless you want her to bleed out?"

"Heal her. She can live in misery the rest of her life, knowing what she almost had."

The guards get moving, but I turn my attention to Ranen, who's under my boot. "Do you have more attacks coming my way?"

He grunts. "Like I'd tell you."

I push my boot down harder.

"I'll talk. I'll talk," he squeaks out. I release some of the pressure, and he says, "There's another attack scheduled for tomorrow while you're at breakfast."

"And who is the attacker?"

He says nothing more, and I press down my boot again.

"A man by the name of Vergul. You'll find him at the Hermit's Bar."

I release him.

"I'll get right on it." Afet leaves the room.

"Stand up," I say.

Ranen groans and curls up.

"Stand up *now*." I want to kick him more than ever. I restrain myself. Somehow.

He struggles to his feet. Did I injure him more than I thought, or is he playing it up?

"Who else are you working with?" I ask.

"No one of consequence." He huffs.

"Not good enough. You will give Wilric every single name if you plan on seeing daylight again after today."

Wilric takes the hint and grabs Ranen by the upper arm. "I'll get everything out of him, Your Majesty. What do you want to happen to them?"

"I decide?" That's not something I want responsibility over if I can help it.

"For a crime like this, yes, it is your decision."

I nod. "Take care to get them all. I don't want more surprises. Ranen is stripped from all titles and holdings. Take him to the dungeon for ten years, then bring him to me. We'll see if he still wants to take my life then. Borkus will share the same fate. And Faya, as soon as she's healed."

Of course, I may not be alive in ten years. I found out who was sending the assassins. That's all I wanted, right?

No. I don't want only that.

I want much more.

CHAPTER 40

Nash rushes to me, in my sitting room.

"I heard what happened," he says. "Are you all right? Do I need to call for a physician?"

"I'm fine." Though I won't stop him from showing concern. It's nice to have someone who cares about your wellness. If only I had such a person in my life sooner.

He stands back. "I'm so happy to hear it. I don't know what I would do if anything happened to you."

I don't want to say it, but it comes out anyway. "You know it's inevitable."

He grips me by both shoulders. Heat blossoms where he touches. "Don't say that. You're far too valuable to be talking that way."

"But it's the way things are, even if I would have them differently." And I do. I want to live. I want to lean in close. To feel him caring for me. To enjoy this world.

But sooner or later, my time will end.

"I will change them." He sounds so certain, I almost believe him.

He lets go of me, and I wish he wouldn't. "Sorry for touching you. It's getting to be a bad habit. You could do something about that. It's in your power to have me killed."

"Like I would do anything of the kind. Your secret is safe with me." He relaxes his face, and I want to tell him how much he means to me. Instead, I clear my throat. "I sent guards to Jem's room. Same for the other ladies in waiting. We are searching for evidence that they were in on Ranen's plot. Since Faya was in on the plot, I trust none of them."

"I spoke to the guards. They should be here soon, to let you know. Do you really think Jem was in on it?"

"More than likely, even if Faya said she was going to control her. The others very well could have been involved too, though. It's hard to say."

"I know you have good reason to distrust them, but some of them do want to help you." His voice is soft.

"Don't you think they just want the crown for themselves?" It feels true.

"Perhaps, but I'd like to think some want what's best for the country. If they see you being a good leader, taking their advice, and thinking of the people, maybe they'll know you are the best option."

There's a knock on the door. Nash answers it and lets in Wilric.

Wilric bows, and I ask, "You have news for me?"

"Yes, Your Majesty. All the rooms were searched, but nothing incriminating was found in any of them. Furthermore, I took it upon myself to search Ranen's and Borkus's rooms. They also revealed no link to the ladies in waiting, though we did find a note in Ranen's room that looked as if it was meant for an assassin."

He hands me the parchment. I look it over to find he indeed wanted to take my life and was requesting someone else do it. Yet again.

I hand back the note. "Please see that it is put somewhere safe, to be used against Ranen."

"Yes, Your Majesty." He bows again before leaving the room.

Nash gives me a look that has my insides melting. I wish he

would touch me again. Make everything all better simply by being near.

He says, "I can't believe Ranen would try to do that to you."

"You mean have me killed?" I don't skirt around the word. "Is it so hard to believe?"

"I suppose not. He's always been a powerful player at court, but I didn't expect him to stoop so low. I hate him for it, but it's not surprising. I guess I just hope for the best in people."

What would he think if he knew who I really was? Would he dislike me as much as he does Ranen? I don't want him to hate me. Just thinking of it shatters my heart.

There's another knock at the door.

"The council wanted to speak with you," Nash says. "There will be someone coming to get us."

"Very well."

I'd much rather stay in my sitting room with his hands on my shoulders. Instead, we head out.

We arrive at the council room, and I take my place at the head of the table. "Why did you wish to speak with me?"

"Your Majesty," Timit says, "we were all so worried over you when we received news of the betrayals."

I'm sure they weren't all worried.

He continues. "After these events, we believe the ball should be canceled."

I narrow my eyes. "Why?"

He looks down. "For your safety, Your Highness."

"My safety, or so you don't have to host poor people?"

He has the grace to turn red.

Kada says, "It's true that we have a hard time understanding why you wanted to host a ball, but we went along with it when we got word. We really are concerned about your safety."

"Forgive me for being the voice of dissension, Your Majesty," Yuka, Head of the Arts says, "but I believe we should go forward with the ball. If we add extra guards, it will be safe, and the people will be happy to have a day of feasting."

Or she could be on Ranen's side and want me out of the way. It's hard to know who to trust.

Kada says, "I disagree. People will not be happy if their queen is murdered before them."

Beside me, Nash tightens his fists.

"No one is going to be murdered," Yuka says. "We will be cautious with our queen. We've dealt with situations where the queen was out in public before. We can do it again."

"Yes, but she wasn't around peasants," Timit says.

I want to growl at him. "If you remember, I was a peasant before I came here," I say.

"But you're not one now," he says. "You are their leader, and as such, you should endeavor to act like it. We've given you time to catch up on the training you should have had before taking the Mortum Tura. Now, you need to be our queen."

Nash bolts to his feet. "You will not talk to Her Majesty that way."

I want to pull him down. To make him stop. But I can't have either him or me looking weak. Plus, he does have a point. They should not speak to me so. I'm glad Nash stood up for me because I'm not certain I could do it for myself in these circumstances.

Timit looks as if he wants to say something more, but I cut him off. "I understand your concerns, but it's best that we go forward."

"Forgive me, Your Majesty," Sidle, the Head of the Military, says, "but I think Timit is right, even if he went too far with his words. It isn't right to put you in danger knowingly."

"I'm in danger every moment of my life." Which hasn't changed by my becoming queen. Some things never do.

"But why should we push that danger?" Sidle asks.

"Because the people need it," I say.

They continue arguing back and forth for the better part of an hour. With my decision made, I let them, without paying them much mind. Sure, the guards could turn on me. The council members might be on Ranen's side. He might have another plan up his sleeve. But I will not give into such tactics.

"Thank you for your opinions," I say. Nash's training has done some good. "I will be going ahead with the ball." They start to speak, but I silence them with a flash of my hand. "This is my final word."

I stand, and Nash does as well.

He follows me out the door. "You handled that well," he says as we walk through the halls. The compliment warms me, but he's not done. "I wonder, though, if it's wise to continue with the ball. I know you want to meet the people and show them you care, but what if someone is waiting to hurt you? We haven't gotten anything else out of Ranen. Whatever reason he had for talking before is no longer a threat. He could have other people on his side."

"I respect your assessment. While I agree somewhat, I feel that we must go on. I can't live my life in fear. I can't let Ranen win by making me go into hiding."

"No, but you could make him win by going out, where he knows you'll be and can hurt you through someone else while you're there."

Is he worried about me as the queen or as something more? I'm brave enough to face murderers, but not to ask if he cares for me. "Everything will be fine. If not, I'll deal with things as they come."

Just like I always do.

CHAPTER 41

"You handled Ranen well." *The first queen's voice comes to me before I see her. When she appears, her face is bright with a smile. "I disliked him from the start."*

"You and me both."

"How did you handle him so well? How did you handle all your attackers?" she asks.

I shrug. "Some people are just good at things."

"Hmm." She stares into my eyes, and I don't look away. "You should have him put to death," she says.

"Do you think so?" The thought makes my hands quiver. It's against the way I was raised to leave someone like him alive. Unless it was Daros. He was never to be harmed.

She moves closer but doesn't reach out to touch me. "I know this is hard for you. I can't pretend to understand why, but you need to do this. He will come back to haunt you if you don't."

He will if I do, too. "He's well tucked away in the dungeons."

"For now. But will he stay that way?"

"I'll put extra guards on him." I'll do anything not to have to give a death sentence.

"Why do you fight so hard against it? Ranen is an evil man."

My throat feels tight, though I'm not awake. "Maybe. Doesn't putting a death sentence on him make me equally evil?"

"Sometimes you have to get rid of an evil man so he doesn't bring an entire nation down."

"Do you think he'd do that?" I know he's bad, but is he that bad?

"I know he would."

"How do you know?"

"Because of past evidence. Ranen has been around for two different queens before you. I know you don't want to hear it, but he manipulated them both."

"But he's imprisoned now. We're safe from him."

"If that is your choice, you should stand by it."

"It is."

He'd better not make me regret it.

CHAPTER 42

THE PREPARATIONS for the ball are coming along nicely. Plenty of food is being prepared in the kitchens and has been for days. The decorations in the ballroom are exquisite, with fabrics in bright colors draped across the walls. The wooden floor is gleaming.

Tonight, I hope to not fall on my face on this floor, in front of the thousand or so people we're expecting. This room won't hold them all, but the palace is big enough that there are plenty of other rooms done up in similar fashion. Throughout the rest of Indell and all of Valcora, similar feasts are being held. My people will hopefully remember this day as a good one.

Inkga comes in the ballroom from a side door. "It's time to get ready for the ball."

"It's not for another three hours," I reply.

"It's not really enough time, but I didn't think you'd let me get away with preparing you all day."

"What could we possibly do that would take so long?"

"Hair. Make up. Perfecting your dress."

"Sounds like nonsense to me."

She laughs. "Maybe, but you want to make a good impression on your guests."

"I suppose." Mostly, I want them to like me, but apparently I'm not that likeable a person. I'll have to figure out another reason for them to like me, other than for who I am.

We move to my bedroom, where my preparatory stuff is waiting, including all five of my other servants. Inkga sits me down and starts by combing through my hair.

"Are you nervous?"

"Of course not." But just in case there's something I can do about it, I ask, "Why do you think so?"

"You're pinching your fingers together."

"Ah." Well, that's easy to fix. If I remember to think about it, that is. I hope I don't do it in the middle of the ball.

After they comb through my short hair, now midway to my ears, and take my hair out of the pins, I make the servants wait in the other room while I take a bath. I put on a shift and open the door for them.

"Why don't you take a seat?" Inkga asks. "We'll get you ready, and then we can put your dress on. There's no sense in wrinkling it or getting it stained."

I take a seat, staring at myself in the vanity. One of the servants takes the mirror off. She turns it around and places it on the floor against the wall.

"Why did you do that?" I ask.

"I asked her to," Inkga says. "I want your final transformation to be a surprise if that's all right, Your Majesty."

"It's fine." Though it's not. I can't see behind me, like I'm used to. I want to know if one of them is about to stab me.

Instead, I'll have to trust them. It's a hard thing to ask of me.

Inkga starts in on my hair, while others work on my nails and face. While my hair is tugged and pulled on, my nails are softened with oil and the tips rounded, and my face is dusted with fine powders—all of which takes a good long while.

I try to sit calmly, but I want to move about. My body aches to get out of this chair, as comfortable as it may be.

A servant comes scurrying in.

"Yes?" I ask.

"Your Majesty, the herald would like to know your name so they can present you properly."

The hands working on me still. This is not something I want to deal with right now. "You don't need to know my name."

"Forgive me, Your Highness, but how will we know what to address you as if we don't know your name?"

Shame burns through me. I keep still. How am I going to get out of this one? "I am Queen of Valcora, that is all the people need to know."

He gives a tight frown and bow before heading back out of the room. My servants continue working on me, their hands moving slower than before. I work to keep from clenching a fist.

When my servants are done, they start in on dressing me in an elaborate silver colored gown. It's made of the silkiest material, almost like water against my skin. They puff and tweak and rearrange.

"There," Inkga says. "You're ready. Would you like to look in the mirror?"

No.

When I don't reply, she says, "Come on. You look fantastic. It's not every night a girl gets to go to a ball, adorned like this."

But what if I hate it? I don't want to hurt her feelings.

"Just look," another girl says.

"You'll love it," says a third.

I haven't heard them so vocal before. Their enthusiasm has me wishing I stopped to learn their names. "I suppose it won't hurt anything to look. But if I don't like it..."

"You will," Inkga says. "I know it."

We spent three hours getting me ready. It's longer than anyone should have to sit in a chair, being primped for something, but I've lived through torture. I can live through this. I might as well see what they've done to me. I take a deep, steadying breath before looking in the mirror they replaced.

My slippers are hidden beneath the volume of fabric. Strands of white swirls are sewn into the silver material. I give a little sway back and forth, letting the skirt swish around my legs. It has a rounded neckline with capped sleeves, and it hugs my thighs, giving me room to walk freely and still hide my daggers.

Though I'm unfashionably skinny, the dress is by far the most beautiful thing I've ever seen. It looks just like it was made for me. If I was into girly things.

My hair is pinned up to look curly around a silver headband that the tiara will go over. My lips are a pale pink, and my cheeks are faintly blushing, but what really gets me is how big and blue my eyes look. They're surrounded by the faintest bit of silvery shimmer.

"It's breathtaking," I say. "Thank you, all."

The girls grin like I rewarded them with extra pay. After this, maybe I will.

"Just in time, too," Inkga says. "The ball is starting now."

I take a deep breath. I suppose it's time. I'm about to attend my first ball. I don't remember ever having such nerves before, except for my first job.

CHAPTER 43

THE WAY IS LONELY, even with my horde of guards and my maids. I wish someone besides them was here to attend me. Well, not any *someone*, but Nash. Having him by my side would make this so much easier. Would he attend me, if I asked him to? He probably would, but I told him I needed to do this part for myself. I need to show the country I am their queen, with no help from others.

Standing on my own is what I do. So what if I happen to want someone with me on occasion?

Two guards and a door stand between me and the ball. The noise of the crowd hums through the wood. I have a surprise waiting for the people, and I can't wait to share it with them.

One of the guards puts his hand on the doorknob but watches me to see when to turn it. I'm hot and crushed inside my dress. I know it's the stress, but it's enough to make me want to go back to my room and hide.

I've never hidden from a challenge, and I'm not about to start now.

I nod to the guard. When he opens the door, a ballroom full of people stop what they are doing to stare at me. I grow even hotter. I step forward, one foot at a time, leading out onto the dais. The guards spread out around me. My servants hang back. There's not a familiar face in all the crush, except my ladies in waiting and the council.

Where is Nash?

"Presenting the Queen of Valcora," a herald announces.

The crowd is so silent, I could whisper and they would hear. As one, they bow to me. I motion for them to rise.

There's an enormous amount of people here. Some in fine ball gowns, others in street clothes—though they look like they did their best to clean up. There's a clear line between the two groups. Though I understand why that separation exists, I wish there was something I could do to eradicate it.

A servant brings me a familiar chalice on a tray. The Mortum Tura. Proof I am the queen.

I grasp the stem and remember the words of the first queen. I need to drink this; it has magic in it. Magic has changed my entire world.

I'm no longer alone.

I reign over a whole country.

I want to live.

Magic has done great things for me. I want more of it. I drink the Mortum Tura until it is all gone.

The crowd watches, eager for the glow that accompanies the famous drink. I don't see it myself—there are no mirrors—but it must start, because there's a collective gasp from the crowd.

They bow again, low to the ground.

They stay there for far too long, even though it's just moments.

Discomfort fills me. "Please, rise."

They stand. Music starts up somewhere. This is not how I expected to feel. I'd much rather be tortured, for this is a torture like no other.

I think about that day that feels so long ago, when I drank the Mortum Tura for the first time. When I speculated on what the cup might be looking for. Now I know it's looking for someone who didn't want the power, but I wonder about the other things.

I may not be the best of souls, but I am trying to be virtuous, to be kind, and to have a clean heart. That I was an assassin doesn't mean I can't be good. The thought fills me with contentment.

Finally, Nash is at my side. Where he came from, I don't know, but he shows up at the perfect time. I wish I could slide my hand into his and hold on tight. A fight is nothing to me, but this amount of people is something else.

I smile at him. And smile at the people around me. And smile at anyone who looks my way. It's a lot of smiling. My cheeks hurt.

Music plays, and dancing begins, but no one asks me to dance as I stand on the dais next to the throne.

Am I that intimidating?

I stop smiling.

Maybe my teeth scared them off? But no. Still no one comes to ask me to dance.

I turn to Nash. "Dance with me."

"I don't know if dancing with your Head Advisor is useful to the image you're trying to create."

"Shut up and dance with me." I grin to soften the words.

He grins. Not the reaction I expected.

"If you command it."

Just want I wanted—to only be danced with because I'm the queen. Oh well. At least I'm not standing any longer.

Nash leads me to the outskirts of the dance floor. The guards clear the way, so no one is close by.

Nash puts his hand near my own. Warmth spills across me, different from the embarrassing heat from before. This is much more pleasant.

The music fades, as do the people around us. It's only me and him.

Nash.

He is everything.

I should have thought of something a while ago. Something I don't know what to do with.

I'm developing strong feelings for him.

"What's wrong?" he asks.

"Why do you assume something is wrong?"

"Because you're shaking."

"Am I?" He can tell that, though we aren't quite touching? The only thing that makes me shake is Daros. How can my nerves be so affected by him?

He narrows his eyes. "You are. What is it?"

I don't know what to say. I don't know what to do. He's supposed to be my advisor. Maybe even a friend. I can't possibly see him as more. How am I going to continue to be around him and not give away my feelings for him?

"I suppose it's nerves."

"From the ball?"

I realize we're dancing in front of people who keep looking my way. Let him think what he wants. I won't lie to him—not about this.

But I can't tell the truth either.

The song isn't nearly long enough after what I realized about how I feel about Nash. I'm not ready to let Nash go. Not ready to face my feelings or the crowd. But all too soon, the music ends, and he leads me to my throne. With a bow, he moves to my side, stoic.

The night wears on, and I spend time talking and eating with people I haven't met before. My guards are close by, not letting anyone pass without being inspected, and keeping it to one person at a time unless a servant is bringing food.

Everyone around me is unfamiliar, except for Nash and my guards, but the latter stay in the distance.

"Ah—my sisters," Nash says as the guards check a couple of girls. "I can't wait to introduce you."

What will they be like? "I'm looking forward to it."

They come forward and curtsy.

"This is Belta." Nash motions to the older girl, who looks about my age. "And this is Lanay."

They both have brown hair, the same color as Nash's. Belta has blue eyes and a bright smile, while Lanay has hazel eyes and a pert nose.

"It's a pleasure to meet you both," I say.

"The pleasure is all ours," Belta replies. "We have been looking forward to this, ever since Nash told us he was your Head Advisor, Your Majesty."

"Even more so since he told us we were to help with the ball," Lanay says.

I didn't realize they were so young. Not that I'm one to talk. "I'm thankful for your service to the crown. This ball wouldn't be nearly as magnificent without your help."

Belta blushes while Lanay beams.

"Is it true you've fought off ten attackers?" Lanay asks, voice eager.

"Lanay, you don't speak to the queen like that," Nash says.

"It's all right," I say. It's refreshing to have someone speak their mind. Even if they're wrong. "I could have fought off ten, but it was only three. And at different times."

Both girls' eyes grow wide.

"Girls," Nash says, "there are others waiting to speak with the queen."

"Of course," Belta says.

They both curtsy again.

"Thank you both again for your help," I say.

"We were happy to assist, Your Majesty," Lanay says.

Together, they make their way out to the dance floor, where they get lost in the crowd.

"I hope they have fun tonight," I say to Nash.

"Not too much fun."

I laugh.

My guards inspect a woman who appears to be in her twenties, young and fresh, with black hair and a bright smile. Though she's wearing a clean dress, it's faded with time and not fancy like the Kurah class's.

After she's cleared, she comes to me and curtsies.

"Please rise," I say.

"Your Majesty, it's such a pleasure to meet you," she says. "I'm here with my grandfather. We're both excited to be given an opportunity to meet our new queen."

"Where is your grandfather?" I ask.

"He's right over there, waiting to speak with you."

I glance at where she's pointing. There's an older gentleman with a cane. Could pose a threat, but I can handle two people if it comes to it. "Send him through," I tell Wilric.

Wilric searches the older man before sending him to me. Despite his age, he bows low to me.

"Rise, good sir," I say.

He does so with a wrinkled smile. "It's an honor to meet you, Your Highness. Thank you for meeting with me and my grand-daughter."

"I'm happy to meet with you."

"We've been anxious to see what changes you are going to make," the woman says.

Brave thing for her to say. "I think you'll like where things are going."

"We already do," the older man says. "In all my days, there hasn't been a queen who's hosted everyone who wanted to come to the palace."

This I didn't know. "I assure you it's a joy to do so. Tell me, what do you do for a living?"

"I'm a seamstress," the woman says. "My grandfather used to be a carpenter."

"My hands got too gnarled to do that job anymore," he says. "But Maly, here, and my daughter take good care of me."

"Is your daughter here as well?" I ask.

He drops his gaze. "No. I'm afraid she didn't want to come."

Ah. I shouldn't dive too deeply there. I don't want him to feel obligated to say something he doesn't want to. "You'll have to take her some food."

"Are you sure, Your Majesty?" Maly asks.

"I'm positive. In fact..." I turn around to the door, where one of my servants waits. "Would you help these good people box up some food to take home?"

She scurries over, ready to help as soon as they are finished speaking with me.

"Thank you, Your Majesty." Maly drops into another curtsy. When she stands again, she adds, "Mother will be pleasantly surprised to hear all that you've said tonight."

"I'm happy to hear it. Please, enjoy yourselves the rest of this evening."

"We will, Your Majesty," the man says.

With a bow, they take their leave.

Nash comes to me. "You're a natural."

Am I? I feel more like a fake, but one who cares. "I want to make a difference in their lives. I don't want them to..." Live like I did, when on the streets. And that wasn't long.

"Don't want them to what?" he asks, looking over the crowd.

"Nothing. I would like to dance with you again before the night is over. No one else seems interested in dancing."

"Give them time. Maybe someone will surprise you."

"Does that mean you're done dancing with me?"

He turns to me with a twinkle in his eye. "Not at all. I'm looking forward to dancing with you again."

My face heats, and there's nothing I can do about it.

He stays at my side as I continue to visit with the people. Old, young, men, women, Poruah class, Medi class, Kurah class—all want a word with me, and most are eager to speak with me. Only a few seem grudging.

"Looks like you have someone else who wants to talk to you," Nash says.

I glance around to find a girl no more than five waiting next in the line of people. She looks up at Nash with expressive green eyes and takes a step back.

"I'll be over here," he says. "Not far at all. Let me know if you need me."

"I will. Thank you."

As soon as he's gone, the little girl walks up to me. She has a doll snug under one arm and wears a tattered but clean dress. I've never known how to handle children. They weren't around at Daros's.

I don't know what to say, but she takes care of it for me. She curtsies—a cute little thing. I tell her she can rise, and she turns those expressive eyes on me.

"Your Majesty," she says with a cute little lisp, "Mama says I shouldn't talk to you, but I want to."

A quick peek around shows a woman waiting near the guards, arms crossed, a scowl on her face, with the same eyes as the girl.

"It's all right," I say. "You can talk to me any time. But we should make it quick, so your mom doesn't worry."

"It's not that she's worried, Your Majesty. It's that she doesn't like queens."

There's honesty. "Oh."

"We came for the food, but you look so pretty in that dress." She eyes the material as if she hasn't ever seen anything so fine.

I don't blame her. Before today, I hadn't either. "Thank you."

"I want you to have this." She holds up her doll to me.

"I couldn't possibly take something so special from you."

"She doesn't get enough to eat with me. I want her someplace like this, where there's lots of food. Somewhere where she'll be protected by guards, like you. She's my bestest friend, and I want you to have her."

The back of my eyelids burn, and my throat closes up. I blink away the tears. How can I tell her *no*? I reach out, and she places the worn and dirty doll in my hand. I bend down to her level and whisper, "I promise to take good care of her."

She nods, runs back to her mother, and wraps her little arms around her mother's leg.

I pull the doll close to my heart as I turn toward one of my servants and motion her over. As soon as she approaches, I whisper, "I want you to discreetly follow that mother and child back to where they live. When you find out, be sure to have an abundance of food delivered to their home, along with a sack of gold."

"Yes, Your Majesty." She gives me a curtsy and moves off into the crowd.

I can't believe that a little girl just gave me her most prized possession. It doesn't seem real. With the doll in my hands and the memory of those expressive eyes, it can't be a dream either.

It's time to be coronated and announce my surprise—I'm lowering taxes. I can't wait to tell them. I'm giddy with excitement. Hopefully this will do some good and put food back on their tables.

I glance at the line to see who's next and whether I feel comfortable putting them off for my coronation and subsequent announcement where I can make the taxes official.

What I see has me wanting to grab my poisoned dagger and run.

My old master.

CHAPTER 44

EVERY STEP DAROS takes toward me has me more frantic on the inside but calmer on the outside. No matter what he says or does now, I'm the queen.

No one told my shaking knees that.

He moves to the guards with his usual confidence. I want to call Afet and Wilric. To make them take him away before he can get to me. He was never supposed to come back to the palace.

But I can't give in like that. Besides, it may make a bigger scene than if I let him say his piece.

If he was here to do more, he wouldn't be doing it in a ballroom.

I think.

I can't be certain. I open my mouth to have him taken out.

"You want to see me," he says, just loud enough that it carries to me. "I have something you need to hear."

Despite my better judgment, my hand waves him through, seemingly on its own. What is going on? It's like even after all this time, he still has me under his control.

After searching him like they've done to others, my guards relax and let him forward. Stupid guards. Don't they know my approval doesn't mean they can stand down? I'll have to have words with them.

If I survive this.

By the time he makes it to me, my knees feel as if they're going to fall off—they're shaking so hard. I can't help it; I sit back on my throne. But I keep my head high.

Daros bows, though there's a mockery in the way he lifts his face and the tightening of his eyes. There's nothing I can do to get rid of him without a scene.

"Your Majesty," he says. "What a pleasant ball you're throwing this evening."

"What are you doing here?" I ask in a low voice.

"Enjoying the party." His voice is loud enough to be heard several people over.

Nash looks him over, his brows furrowed as he stares at Daros. If I give him a signal, he'll be over here in an instant, but I have to fight my battles alone.

Besides, I don't want Nash to hear whatever Daros is going to say.

I turn back to my old master. "Is it to your liking, then?" I keep the quiver from my voice quite nicely.

"This is the best party I've been to." His grin makes me even more uneasy. What is he up to? "Tell me, Your Majesty, how well do the people know you?"

With growing trepidation, I say, "Not well enough, which is why I'm hosting this ball."

"I also find it the perfect opportunity to have them get to know you better."

My guards are looking between him and me. Maybe I should appear more friendly, or he should act less so.

"They're already getting to know me better just by being here," I say. "I don't think anything else is necessary."

"Oh, but I disagree."

"Don't." I try to keep my face clear of emotion. Smooth. Calm. But I'm roiling inside. Tossing and turning with fear. Why is he threatening to out me here? Does he really want the whole country

JANEAL FALOR

to know who I am? They can't know. They'll have me killed and then search for a new queen within an instant.

"Things might be different if you hadn't turned me away when I came to visit you before."

"I broke off all ties with you when I left your house. My becoming the queen doesn't change things." I fiddle with the dagger just inside the seam of my pocket.

He leans in close, his face an inch from mine. "It changes everything."

"Perhaps we should discuss this elsewhere."

"This is the ideal place to discuss what you're like."

The people closest to us stop and stare.

"Don't," I say again, voice loud and firm.

"You don't want me to?" For once, his voice is quiet. Barely audible. "Do what I tell you to do."

My chest constricts. "And what is that?"

"I will become your new Head Advisor, and you will do exactly what I want. No questions. No running away. Simply following my instructions. If you don't... Well, then, I'll have to proceed with the unfortunate business of telling them who you are."

I clench my jaw. "You wouldn't dare."

"As it happens, I would. I have a witness, willing to come forward and back up my words should I not be believed. You are nothing against me."

It makes my stomach roil to realize I'm considering what he asks. After a lifetime of following him, how can I refuse?

Yet, how can I not?

"You've got five seconds to decide. If you choose wrong, everyone here will know what you are and what you have done."

No. That's not enough time. I can't do this. I can't go back under his rule. But I can't have everyone turn on me either.

"Two seconds," he says.

It feels as if someone is choking me. I don't know what to do. I don't want to be his puppet again.

Lost.

Alone.

Controlled.

"Time's up." He scowls.

"I will do as you ask." The words are torn from me, shattering my soul.

"Good. First thing you will do is dismiss your Head Advisor and name me your new one." When I don't respond, he says, "Right now."

I glance at Nash. How can I go on without him? He's turned into my best friend. I don't know if he considers me the same, but I'm closer to him than I've ever been to anyone.

I want him in my life.

I need him.

"No." The sound jumps out of me.

"What did you say?" Daros's voice is menacing as ever.

"No. I won't do it. You can say what you will about me, but you will never again control me."

He smirks.

"Nash," I call out.

Before I can say anything further, Daros turns to the room. "Your queen is a murderer. An assassin, sent to kill the last queen."

A gasp echoes through the crowd. Some look disbelieving, but many turn accusing gazes on me.

Despite my fear, I stand, holding my head high.

The people back farther away in a surge. Even the guards.

"You weren't meant to govern," Daros tells me. "It's time you let someone else take over who knows how to do the job properly." Someone he can control, he means.

"You can never rule this country. That's my job," I say.

He comes at me. Who knows his intentions? Either he wants to knock some sense in me to get me under his thumb or he wants to kill me. But I won't let him.

I strike first, throwing a dagger at him before he can reach me. It enters his shoulder, but still he comes at me, even with no weapon in hand. It takes more than a scratch to stop him, even if that was my poisoned dagger. He's immune to the venom. It would take more than I have to drop him. I'm not going to defeat him.

As he comes closer, I pull out a second dagger with a slash and thrust, cutting him again. He knocks my hand aside, pulls the blade out of his shoulder, and goes for my gut. I block him with my other hand. Blood seeps from his wound, but it's not enough to stop him.

My guards stare at the fight like they don't know if they should join in or not. Even Afet and Wilric are looking at me aghast. I can't see Nash anywhere. Maybe he abandoned me the moment he heard.

I pull out my knife and dodge back to my throne. Something hits it as I dive behind it. I push out fast the same side I came, catching him by surprise. There are several screams from those gathered. Boots stomp closer. Afet and Wilric finally come around, but they won't reach me in time.

Soon, this will all be over.

I fight hard. With all my power. And yet, his little effort feels like more. He's tougher than I am. I can see it in his eyes. He taught me everything I know, but he didn't teach me everything he knows.

My daggers are useless, my poison useless. All I have is the knowledge he gave me. There has to be more. More I can use to get out of this.

I have to be quick. Faster than him. Faster than me.

It doesn't matter.

I can't win.

I'm going to die. But not without taking him with me.

I give it everything, pouring myself into the fight like I've never done before. The first queen's presence is near, hoping for my victory and life. Whether it's because I just drank the Mortum Tura or because of the danger to my life or perhaps some other reason, I don't know.

But it's not to be. Heedless of my safety, I slash at him. He drops, avoiding my dagger. He swings a blade at my legs, but I manage to kick it out of his hands, for once being faster than him. I have the high ground for the only time I can ever remember. Where this power flowing through me is coming from doesn't matter. It only matters that I finally have power to defeat him.

I hover over him. My win is imminent, but it's harsh. Cold. Whatever I do to him, there is a certain part of me he'll always have a hold over. No matter what happens, that part of me won't ever recover. It will be wounded by him even if I win.

"An assassin was never meant to be queen," Daros says.

"And yet, a queen I am."

I move to stab him in the heart. Just before I sink my knife to the hilt, I stop myself. I promised not to kill for any reason.

It's a promise I can't break, even now.

I put the blade to his throat. "Never again will you have power over me."

CHAPTER 45

THE PARTY IS OVER, to say the least.

People go home, taking their shock with them. I'm not certain how many of them believe Daros's words, but I do know this has left them with a bad impression of me.

I stalk over to where several guards have Daros restrained, his wound bound. I don't want to face him. I want to turn and run in the opposite direction. But there are some things I have to know. Fleeing is not an option.

"Why did you have me kill the previous queen?" I demand of him.

He sneers.

I want to whip out a blade and place it against his throat, but I'm stronger than that. "Tell me."

"The same reason I've always had you kill people. She was in my way, insisting on things I didn't want. You think I can afford all my nice things while being under heavy taxes?"

I stare at him. I didn't expect a response. "All this was about taxes?"

"Among other things." He smirks.

It's odd that he's bound and restrained by my guards, yet so smug. "Who were you going to put on the throne?" I ask.

His smile fades. "Not you."

That much is obvious. "Who, then?"

He clamps his mouth closed, in the way that means he's done talking. I've seen it too many times before. At least I got a little bit of an answer out of him. I wish I could give him whatever made Faya run her mouth, but it's not to be.

"Take Daros away," I tell the guards, but I don't notice their reactions in my daze.

Usually, I have a lot of energy after a fight. Not tonight. I'm drained. Even my thoughts are muddled.

I wind up back in my sitting room, with Nash at my side. After everything, he's the last person I want to see.

"Is it true?" he asks. "Are you really an assassin?"

"It's true." What is he going to think of me now?

His chest rises with a slow, deep breath. The quiet stretches between us. Finally he says, "Why didn't you tell me?"

Why didn't I? I had opportunities. I should have spoken up. I care about him as more than just a friend, after all.

More than that, I trust him. Really trust him.

So much so that I'm willing to tell him the truth. "Because I'm embarrassed by my past. I wish I never was an assassin, but it's what I was raised to do. It was all I knew. Daros brought me up. He taught me everything I know. It's hard to think of anything outside of what he drilled into me."

"Tell me one thing. Did you truly kill the Queen Deedra?"

Those eyes come to me again, haunting and clear, right before I stabbed her. I blink to rid my eyes of their sudden moisture. When I speak, my voice is small. "I did."

He looks far off, to something I can't see.

I wish I knew what he was thinking—if he's going to reject me, now that he knows the truth. Is he going to leave me? Refuse to be my Head Advisor? Refuse anything to do with me?

No one can take away being queen from me; that much has been proven by the past. But it doesn't mean the people can't hate me. Revile me. Push me away. Try harder for my death.

Is that what he wants now?

I have to say something. I have to try to keep him with me, even if my efforts are doomed to fail. "I didn't want to. I didn't know I had a choice. It wasn't until afterward that I realized I could stand up to Daros. The feelings I had when I..." How do I say *killed the queen*? When I snuck in her bedroom and stabbed her in the heart, right between the ribs. My stomach roils. "During the last job made me realize how wrong it was. How horrid of a thing. I'd felt guilt before, but never as strongly as with the last queen. I knew I was affecting an entire nation and it was something I shouldn't have any control over.

"I knew when I took her life that it was wrong. The way she looked at me..." I shudder. "The look in her eyes haunts me. As soon as I killed her, I knew I made a mistake. Knew something had to be done about it. I stood up to Daros. Ran away. Most of all, I promised never to kill again. It was by far the most frightening thing I've ever done, but I stick by it.

"Then, while I was on the streets, I thought about everything I'd done. Everything I was. The more I thought, the less I felt like living. I'd killed innocent people—done what Daros told me to do, no matter that it was because he tortured me if I didn't. I was ashamed of myself. I regretted everything I came to stand for. I wanted to end my life. That's why I took the Mortum Tura—to end my life in a way that I would be remembered in dying, even if I didn't have a name. I never expected to become queen."

That's it. If he leaves me, I'll know I tried.

He faces me, expression flat for a brief moment, before he takes my hand. "You can tell me anything. Please don't feel like you have to hide something from me just because you're embarrassed."

My heart skips a beat. "Do you mean that?"

"I do."

"Then there's something else I should tell you."

"What is it?"

"I care about you."

He pulls me close. He smells of metal and earth. "I care about you too. And as more than my queen."

The next thing I know, we're kissing. His lips on mine. Mine on his. It's like a magic I've never known before. Warmth swirls around me, making me want him closer. I wrap my arms around him and press him near.

For the first time I can remember, my heart swells with passion. I want to be there for him. To help him however I can. I want to keep him safe.

As the kiss deepens, so do my feelings. It's like allowing myself to finally feel something lets me open up. I need him. And from the way he's kissing me back, he needs me too. There's an energy here I haven't felt before.

His lips are hungry, his fingers eager for me. I'm just as eager for the taste of him. The feel of him. Everything I ever wanted is right here. Right now. I won't ever have enough of this.

Telling him was cleansing. He makes me feel like being a better person. Like wanting to do right by him and my people.

When we pull apart, I'm breathless.

I lean my head on his shoulder and breathe him in. Unbidden thoughts of how this is against the law consume me, but I shove them away. There will be time to think of such things later. For now, I want to enjoy his company.

"I think it's time we give you a name," he says. "You more than deserve one."

I hum, happy to be near him, but also at the thought of getting a name. Being called something. Having something that belongs to me and no one else.

"What do you think it should be?" I ask.

"That's for you to decide."

"I get to pick myself?" The thought isn't one I've had before. I've always been *girl* or now *Your Majesty*, *My Lady*, and *Your Highness*. It's all too much and seems nothing like me.

What is me?

Nothing frilly. Not soft or sweet. Fun, but with an edge.

"What do you think of the name Ryn?" I ask.

"I think it suits you."

"Ryn. My name is Ryn."

AFTERWORD

If you enjoyed reading this book, please consider helping the author by leaving a review where you purchased the book and/or on Goodreads. Even a simple one line review helps.

You can sign up to receive notification when Janeal Falor releases a new book at www.janealfalor.com with a Release Notification link on the side bar. Or talk to the author directly at janealfalor@gmail.com

ACKNOWLEDGMENTS

This book has been in my heart for so long, I'm grateful to finally have it out there, and it wouldn't have happened without some special people.

I had an amazing set of beta readers this go around. Kallista Foote gave tons of good feedback on how to expand and develop the story. Jessie Wolf had a good eye for things plus great comments and insights. Danielle Lori caught lots of typos (which I'm forever making) and gave me thoughts on the books that helped. Samantha Armstorng gave very thorough notes helping me expand and solidify the story. Alexis Jones also helped me see where I needed to expand, giving good thoughts, and helping me feel good about the book. Thank you so much to all of you. This book would be much sadder without you!

For my many errors I had lots of assistance, though if any remain I take full responsibility. Sotia Lazu, thank you for everything. You fixed up my mess of a first draft, helped me figure out what was wrong, and more importantly, how to fix it. Then, you gave it a thorough sweep through when it was ready for a copy edit. This book would not exist without you. Best editor ever!

Erin Kasper took the time to let me know the grammar errors she found in the first chapter without even being asked. This was helpful and very sweet! Alex Richardson also took the time to point out the grammar errors she found so I could fix them. Your rock!

Yesenia Vargas is my awesome proofreader, plus she pointed out the last few touches that needed to be made. Thanks, Yesenia! Cynthia Shepp did something incredible. She helped with my blurb. I'm horrible at writing these things, but she did a fantastic job of pulling it together.

The cover that I so dearly love was made by the fabulous Lou Harper. Thank you so much for taking the time to put up with my pickiness and giving me the cover of my dreams.

The biggest thanks of all goes to my family. They put up with a lot of rough times that inspired this book, not only put up with them, but helped me through them with love and care. Tai, Xandria, and Will, you three are the best ever! I don't know what I would do without your sweet influences in my life. And my sweet Erik. There aren't words enough to express what I feel for you. You've not just stuck by me through thick and thin, you patiently helped me through it, always loving me. You are my everything. I love you with the depths of my soul. Thank you.

ABOUT THE AUTHOR

Amazon best selling author Janeal Falor lives in Utah with her husband and three children. In her non-writing time she teaches her kids to make silly faces, cooks whatever strikes her fancy, and attempts to cultivate a garden even when half the things she plants die. When it's time for a break she can be found taking a scenic drive with her family or drinking hot chocolate.

For more information:
www.janealfalor.com
janealfalor@gmail.com